GRATEFUL LADY

The first time Fargo saw Blossom Daley, he saved the voluptuous blond beauty from rape by a lusting Apache band. The second time, he saved her from rape again—this time from a pair of sex-starved range bums.

"I know you're thinking I ought to do something about being grateful," she told him.

"You're half right," said Fargo.

"What does that mean?" asked Blossom.

"I mean being grateful isn't the only reason for doing things. Just wanting to is enough."

"I don't know enough about you yet," she said.

"Ask," said Fargo.

"No, I'll find out my own way," she said, as she lifted her arms to encircle his neck, and let him feel her firm, proud breasts pressing against him.

Blossom might have been twice-burnt—but now it was Skye Fargo who was playing with fire. . . .

Exciting Westerns by Jon Sharpe

THE TRAILSMAN 43

MESQUITE MANHUNT

by
Jon Sharpe

Ø
A SIGNET BOOK

NEW AMERICAN LIBRARY

PUBLISHER'S NOTE

This novel is a work of fiction. Names, characters, places, and
incidents either are the product of the author's imagination or
are used fictitiously, and any resemblance to actual persons,
living or dead, events, or locales is entirely coincidental.

Copyright © 1985 by Jon Sharpe

All rights reserved

The first chapter of this book previously appeared in
Renegade Command, the forty-second volume in this series.

 SIGNET TRADEMARK REG. U.S. PAT. OFF. AND FOREIGN COUNTRIES
REGISTERED TRADEMARK—MARCA REGISTRADA
HECHO EN CHICAGO, U.S.A.

SIGNET, SIGNET CLASSIC, MENTOR, PLUME, MERIDIAN AND
NAL BOOKS are published by New American Library,
1633 Broadway, New York, New York 10019

First Printing, July, 1985

1 2 3 4 5 6 7 8 9

PRINTED IN THE UNITED STATES OF AMERICA

The Trailsman

Beginnings . . . they bend the tree and they mark the man. Skye Fargo was born when he was eighteen. Terror was his midwife, vengeance his first cry. Killing spawned Skye Fargo, ruthless, cold-blooded murder. Out of the acrid smoke of gunpowder still hanging in the air, he rose, cried out a promise never forgotten.

The Trailsman, they began to call him, all across the West: searcher, scout, hunter, the man who could see where others only looked, his skills for hire but not his soul, the man who lived each day to the fullest, yet trailed each tomorrow. Skye Fargo, the Trailsman, the seeker who could take the wildness of a land and the wanting of a woman and make them his own.

*1861—the New Mexico Territory,
where the other word for savagery
was Apache. . . .*

1

Dammit, he should never have agreed to do it, the big man reprimanded himself as he inched his way along-side the jagged rocks. The full moon bathed the mesa in a silver light that outlined every sandstone pinnacle and butte as well as the six figures grouped around the small fire. They sat in the clear flatland, a dozen yards from the line of rocks that marched along one side of the mesa. Apache, of course, the big man muttered to himself. Their long, black, stringy hair, brow bands, and short-legged Indian ponies had told him that much. But he needed to know more, and once again he swore at himself for being there.

He inched forward again and felt the loose, sandy soil dig into his naked abdomen. Except for B.V.D.s and his gun belt, he was stark-naked, his clothes back with the Ovaro where he'd left the horse on the other side of the line of rocks. He inched forward a little more and paused. A soft, warm wind blew across the mesa and he could hear the sound of the Apache talk-ing in low, half-grunted sentences. Again he edged forward along his belly and suddenly froze as he heard the loose sand move almost directly in front of him, the little pebbles not so much dislodged as rubbed against one another in a soft, slithering sound.

Shit, Fargo murmured inwardly as he watched the snake slip around the edge of a hedgehog cactus. The red, yellow, and black bands, unmistakable even in

9

the pale light of the moon, marked it as a coral snake, as deadly as it was beautiful. A distant relative of the cobra, the coral snake was a nervous reptile. There'd be no coiling up before striking, no warning rattle, only an instant, darting flash that would make the red, yellow, and black into a blur of color.

Fargo's hand lay against his side, his fingertips touching the butt of the big Colt .45 in the holster. The snake slid forward, slowed, its forked tongue darting out to read the air. Fargo's lips pulled back in a tight grimace. If he had time to blow the snake away, the Apache would be on him in moments. The old saying fit too damn well, he grunted: he was between a rock and a hard place.

He watched through slitted eyes as the coral snake slithered closer, moved only a half-foot from his bare shoulder, the forked tongue constantly darting out, detecting the heat of his body. Fargo's fingers closed around the butt of the big Colt. The deadly snake moved, its tongue flicking out almost too quickly to see, and suddenly, out of the corner of his eye, Fargo glimpsed the small, scurrying shape, tan on top, snowy white on the underside of its jaw, throat, and chest. He recognized the small, desert dweller as a white-throated wood rat, and he saw the snake suddenly change direction, slide across the ground with astonishing speed. The wood rat had given off a more concentrated area of heat and the serpent had fixed on it instantly. Fargo held motionless as he watched the coral snake disappear into the rocks after the rodent.

He let a sigh of relief blow through his lips in a slow hiss and he felt the wetness of his palms. Slowly, he wiped his hands along his legs and wrenched his attention back to the figures beside the fire. The six Apache continued to relax casually in the warm night, and grimacing, Fargo again inched his near-naked body over the dry, sandy soil. He kept to the edge of the jagged line of rocks. He'd have to leave their deep shadows to crawl closer along the open ground, he knew, but he'd wait till the Apache fell asleep. He halted finally, pressed himself against the stones in the black shadows. He'd come as close as he dared without moving into the open, and he settled his powerfully muscled body into the shadows to wait, his chiseled handsomeness drawn tight.

He muttered silently at himself again and let his thoughts unwind backward. Old friends and old favors, that's why he was here, he growled inwardly, and his thoughts leapt back to the army post just north of the Rio Hondo, base of the Forty-first United States Cavalry Troop. The regiment was commanded by Maj. Thomas Carpenter, army career man, top-drawer field commander, and old friend. Tom Carpenter was the only reason he was here in the New Mexico Territory lying near-naked under a full moon trying to get too damn close to six Apaches.

He could've turned down Tom Carpenter, Fargo grimaced, but then he'd never been much for turning his back on old obligations. There was a time he'd never forget, when the major had backed him with half a regiment in an effort to box in one of the men he'd hunted to avenge the wiping out of his family. It seemed so long ago now and it had been the wrong man, but that didn't matter. What mattered was that Tom Carpenter had bent army regulations to help, had understood, had stuck his own neck out. And now he was the one in a bind and needing help. Besides, the major had offered three times the usual scout's pay, and it was a sin to turn down that kind of money. Fargo smiled wryly. That afternoon only a week ago in Tom Carpenter's office had been spent over a bottle of bourbon and a sack of memories.

But the reminiscences had come to an end and the major had leaned forward, his long face even more

11

drawn than usual, his graying hair somehow more gray. "Fargo, I'm like a damn cornstalk in the wind out here," he'd said. "I'm supposed to keep this whole New Mexico Territory in hand with one lousy regiment. You know what this place is, Fargo. The Spaniards couldn't handle it, the Mexicans were glad to get rid of it, and the Indians never gave it up. Now they want me to go find somebody the Apaches captured a month ago."

"That means somebody dead by now," Fargo had offered.

"Likely, but important people say maybe not. They want proof, and I'm getting a lot of pressure," the major had said.

"Pressure? Important people?"

"Such as United States Senator Robert Talbot," the major said, and Fargo remembered his brows lifting. "The man he wants me to find is his brother, Dale Talbot." Fargo's brows had lifted further. "The senator and his party will be here next week," the major had gone on. "Of course, he doesn't know the first goddamn thing about this murderous, varmint-infested territory they're calling New Mexico. He thinks I'm going to wave a magic wand and have some answers for him. Hell, I know that's damn near impossible, but I've got to make a stab at it. I've got to show him I've tried. That's where you come in, Fargo. If there's anything to find, you can find it."

"Out of nowhere? I just pick a direction and start looking?" Fargo protested.

Tom Carpenter's laugh had been grim. "It's bad, but not that bad. Talbot had three men with him when the Apache hit. One, a boozy old guide named Johnny Kelter, managed to hide and stay alive. He told us where they hit Talbot. It's a jumping-off place for you. If you can just find out which Apaches took him, that'll be something I can wave at the good senator when he gets here, which will be next week sometime."

"That means you're giving me a week to get back with something," Fargo had said.

"I know, that's pretty impossible. Do the best you can, that's all," Tom Carpenter had said, and had given him the few facts he had. A handshake had been all that was needed after that, and Fargo thought about how he'd set off at once for the foothills of the Sacramento Mountains where Dale Talbot had been captured.

The Trailsman broke off his thoughts as one of the Apache stood up, then another, and he drew his attention back to them. As he watched, the six Indians stirred, changed positions as the fire burned low. They were preparing to bed down, he saw with grim satisfaction. He had picked up the six south of Cactus Creek and stayed well back until they'd halted for the night on the mesa. His plan was to put five of them out while they slept. Hardly sporting, but the Apache would think nothing of slitting a man's throat while he slept. He needed only one awake to question. The Apache all spoke one or another dialect of the Athapaskan language, and he'd enough working familiarity with the tongue to serve him.

Fargo pushed himself up on one elbow as the Indians began to lie down in a half-circle around the embers of the little fire. They'd sleep quickly. Indians seldom tossed and turned. He let his gaze drift out across the mesa, travel along the black shadows of the line of rocks where he lay and, beyond the rocks, the foothills of the Sacramento Mountains touched by the moon's pale glow.

His eyes returned to the Indians. Two were still settling themselves, the others already turned on their sides to sleep. Suddenly, as he watched with an instant frown, all six of the Apache leapt to their feet with quick, catlike motions. He saw them freeze in place, listening, two with bone hunting knives drawn, their eyes searching the dark shadows of the rocks.

Goddamn, Fargo swore silently. He hadn't done anything to set them off, and the frown dug deeper into his forehead as he saw the Indians begin to move forward with cautious steps. With quick, silent, catlike movements, the six figures headed for the rocks. While he stared, they spread out and, as if galvanized into action, raced forward to the rocks only a few dozen yards from where he lay. He pushed himself up to a crouch, the big Colt .45 in his hand. What the hell had happened? he wondered, and frowned into the night as he heard them scrambling up the rocks.

He strained his eyes, but the shadows were too deep for him to see anything, yet he heard one of the Apache shout, another answer, and then a woman's voice, a half-scream quickly drowned out by more triumphal shouts of the Apache.

Fargo stayed motionless and saw the Indians come into sight again, two dragging the figure between them while the others half-ran, half-leapt excitedly alongside. They reached the almost-burned-out fire and flung the woman to the ground. Fargo could see only a slender figure and long hair that hung loose and very blond even in the pale moonlight. The young woman got to her feet and aimed a sweeping blow at the nearest Indian; the Apache twisted away and brought a short left under the girl's swing. It caught her in the pit of the stomach, and Fargo heard her gasp of pain as she fell to her knees. The Indian seized the long blond tresses and yanked, and the young woman went sprawling facedown on the ground.

Fargo felt his finger tighten on the trigger of the Colt, and he forced his hand to relax. Another of the Apache leapt atop the young woman as she lay on her stomach. He threw her skirt up over her waist and

14

Fargo glimpsed the rounded, full rear under the pink bloomers the Indian started to rip down.

Damn, Fargo swore as his finger tightened on the trigger again, but another Apache, a tall, lanky figure, seized the Indian atop the girl and yanked him off. Fargo heard his shout of command and the other Indian's angry answer as they faced each other. The others joined in and Fargo picked up the core of the argument. The lanky-figured one seemed to be the leader, and he ordered the girl to be brought back to their camp while the others were divided about enjoying her right there and then. But the lanky one was adamant. "No," Fargo heard him insist with authority. "We take her back first, let Huanco find out why she spy on us." Fargo heard the others grumble but the name of their chief seemed to have a quickly quieting effect as they backed down at once.

The lanky-figured Apache stepped to where the girl had pulled herself to her knees, and he motioned to one of the others. The man brought him a length of rawhide, and with rough, harsh motions he tied her wrists and ankles. With another long piece of rawhide he made a leash from her wrists to his hand and moved away from the girl. Fargo saw him wrap the leather around his left wrist as he sat down on the ground. The Indian yanked hard and the girl pitched forward almost onto her face. "Lay down. Sleep," Fargo heard the Indian bark. The girl didn't need to know the language to get the message, and Fargo saw her stay on the ground, turn on her side, and grow quiet. The others had stretched out again and started to return to sleep, he saw, and as the soft night wind drifted across the mesa, Fargo had the answer to one question . . . but only one.

He peered at the young woman, watched her turn on her back and let the long, thick blond hair form a pillow under her head. Who was she? he frowned.

More important, what the hell was she doing up in the rocks? Had she been lost, wandering around aimlessly? Or had she been watching the six Apache, too? He swore in silent anger. Who, why, or whatever, she had thoroughly ruined his chance to sneak up closer to the six Apache. He'd have to crawl across the open land and she'd be sure to see him as he neared. She'd make some move—out of surprise, if nothing else—and the one with the rawhide around his wrist would be awake instantly, the others only a half-second later, and he'd be caught on his belly out in the open. He'd nail some of them, but they were too spread out for him to get them all.

Damn her hide, Fargo swore as he sat back against the rocks and let thoughts pull at him. Not only had she wrecked his plans, but he couldn't see himself just leaving her to the Apache. Again he wondered where the hell she'd come from in the night. He angrily shook away speculation about her and forced his mind to pull at other avenues to save her hide and, hopefully, to get the answers he wanted from the Apache. The Indians fell asleep as Fargo let his thoughts continue to turn. He saw the girl move restlessly, and each time she did, the Indian with the rawhide on his wrist woke at once to yank hard in reprimand and she lay still.

As the moon began to slide down the far side of the night sky, Fargo pulled himself to his feet, his lips drawn back in a grimace. He'd come up with only one plan that had a chance of succeeding, and it counted on typical Apache behavior.

He began to pull himself up higher on the rocks at his back, climbing with the silent grace of a mountain cougar. Reaching the top of the rocks, he hunkered his near-naked frame between two tall rocks that let him look down on the Apache and afforded him cover at the same time. That was all-important. If they saw him, they'd rush him no matter what kind of barrage he laid down. But they wouldn't rush him if he stayed unseen behind the rocks. The Apache didn't like the unknown. They wouldn't rush blindly at what they couldn't see or weren't reasonably certain about. It was their way, their own combination of bravery and prudence, cunning and caution.

He settled himself down and watched the first streaks of dawn spread across the sky. As the day began to lighten the dark, he took the Colt from its holster, rested it atop the rocks, and drew a bead on the sleeping figures below. He was poised and ready as the new day moved over the mesa and he saw the tall Apache wake first, get to his feet, and unwind the length of rawhide from his wrist. Fargo watched the young woman push herself up, and for the first time he had a proper look at her. He saw a gray shirt pulled tight around a tall, slender figure, the long, thick hair wheat-gold in the new sun. He could make out a straight, thin nose and even features in an unquestionably attractive face. As the other Indians rose, one moved toward her and she instantly aimed a kick at him. He twisted away from the kick and caught her with a blow that hit her in the side. She grimaced, but her angry glare didn't change. Maybe she was afraid, but she was hard-nosed enough to tough it out, he noted.

Fargo leaned forward. The time had come. He aimed, let his finger slowly tighten on the trigger, a gentle pressure that would keep the Colt from bucking. The shot split the air and one of the Indians fell with a half-scream of pain, clutched at his leg with one hand as the others spun, their eyes searching the rocks.

Fargo called out in the Apache tongue. "Listen or you die," he said. "Many guns here." He watched the tall Apache scan the rocks with narrowed, probing black eyes. One of the others suddenly broke, raced for their ponies tethered to the side. Fargo fired again, no leg shot this time, and the Indian twisted, pitched forward, and lay still. Fargo saw the others remain frozen, their eyes on the rocks. "Bring the girl," he called. The others shot quick glances at the tall, lanky-figured one, who remained in a half-crouch. Fargo emphasized his words with a shot that sent a spray of dirt flying into the air at the edge of the Indian's right foot.

The Apache pushed the girl forward and followed her as she approached and halted at the base of the line of rocks. Fargo saw the Indian's black eyes darting back and forth up the jagged rocks as he tried to see through the narrow crevices in the stones. The Indian probably didn't buy the remark about many guns, Fargo realized, but he wasn't certain and, more important, the Apache knew he was an open target. "You take white man one moon ago," Fargo called from behind the rocks.

"No," the Indian grunted, and Fargo, peering from behind the narrow crevice, saw the girl frowning up at the rocks.

"You take white man, kill him," Fargo said, and the Indian shook his head again. Fargo fired a bullet that creased the brow band along the side of the Apache's head. The man flinched but his face remained set.

"No," the Indian repeated.

"You hear? You know?" Fargo asked.

The Indian shook his head again, his face a sullen mask.

Fargo grunted silently. He hadn't really expected an answer. If the Indian did know anything, he wouldn't be answering without a lot of pain and torture, but the questions had given him the time to study the man and he cursed softly. The Apache had no design on his moccasins, no necklace, no embroidered brow band, not even a beaded armband to mark him. But maybe that said something of itself, Fargo reflected. He lifted his voice again. "White Mountain?" he called, and saw the Apache nod. Fargo waited a long moment before he spoke again. "Leave the girl," he ordered, and saw the Apache peer intently up at the rocks. The Indian stayed, thoughts racing behind his angry black eyes. "Leave the girl," Fargo said again, and put more sharpness into his voice.

The Apache delayed another half-minute before he turned, deciding to leave with his skin intact. He walked slowly to the ponies and the others started to follow, the one limping along on his wounded leg. They dragged the dead one with them and draped him over one of the ponies, and Fargo saw the tall Apache mount a spotted pony and stare back at the rocks for a long moment. He was still trying to see a way to attack, and Fargo helped him make up his mind by firing a quick shot that whistled only inches over the Indian's head. The Apache turned his pony and galloped off across the mesa.

Fargo stayed in place and glanced down at the girl as she watched the Indians until they were out of sight. He waited and she turned to look up at the rocks, a frown across her brow. He saw very blue eyes that were as sharp as they were bright, full red lips under the straight nose, flat cheekbones, and a long, graceful neck that seemed terribly white against the wheat-gold hair. Modest breasts sat firmly under the gray shirt, he noted.

"Climb up here, honey," he called, then stood up and reloaded the Colt as he watched her pull her way slowly up the side of the rocks. He was waiting as she reached the top and leapt lightly down to the flat space beneath the jagged topline, and he saw her very blue eyes widen in surprise. She swept her glance up and down his powerfully muscled tall frame, the tight

19

B.V.D.s, which left little to the imagination, and only the gun belt over them.

"Who are you, and what the hell were you doing up here in these rocks last night?" he asked.

Her eyes lingered on his crotch and then moved across his body again. "What the hell kind of an outfit is that?" she muttered.

"The kind of an outfit that just saved your little ass, honey," Fargo growled impatiently. "Start talking."

Her eyes flicked up and down his body again. "No," she said. "I'm not telling anything to anybody who goes around dressed like that."

2

Fargo stared at the girl in disbelief. "You know what I'm thinking?" he growled.

"Tell me," she said firmly.

"I'm thinking maybe I should've left you to those Apache," he snapped.

The very blue eyes didn't waver. "And I'm thinking maybe I've gone from the frying pan into the fire," she said, and her glance flicked over his near-nakedness again.

"I've clothes, dammit. They're back with my horse," Fargo said.

"Prove it," she returned.

"Damn, you've more sass than a jug of year-old corn liquor." Fargo frowned.

"You look at yourself and you wouldn't say that," she returned.

Fargo's lake-blue eyes stayed hard, but her answer jabbed at him. His attire certainly would raise eyebrows, he realized, and maybe her reaction was to be expected. "All right," he grunted. "I'll get my clothes and you better be ready to talk. Let's go."

"No, my horse is on the other side of the rocks. I'll wait there for you," she said.

He cast a narrowed glance at her, but her face stayed aloofly adamant. He pulled himself up on the higher rocks at his back and looked down the other side. He saw a gray horse, a big, heavy-legged mount,

21

probably standardbred in him, sturdy enough to easily carry the extra pack she had strapped over his croup. Fargo slid down to the girl and saw her eyes move over his muscled frame again.

"Satisfied?" she asked tartly.

"I'll come around the back side of the rocks and meet you at your horse," he muttered. She nodded, and he felt her eyes following him as he began to climb along the line of rocks. He lowered himself to the small rocks near the start of the stone formation as it grew up from the edge of the mesa, and he soon came into sight of the Ovaro, the horse's jet-black fore and hind quarters and pure white midsection gleaming in the sun. Taking off his gun belt, he pulled his clothes from where he'd tied them across the saddle, quickly dressed, put his gun belt back on, and swung up on the horse. He steered the Ovaro around the end of the rocks and out along the back side of the formation, put the horse into a canter along the line of stone until he reached the place where he said he'd meet the girl.

But only the emptiness of the mesa met his eyes and he felt his lips pull tight. "Little bitch," he bit out as he gazed across the back of the mesa. She's fled—probably never intended to wait for me to return, he thought. What the hell was she all about? he wondered as he took in the hoofprints in the loose, sandy soil. She'd gone northwest in a full gallop and seemed headed for the Sacramento Mountains not more than a few miles away. He ought to just write her off as some strange, maybe frightened, crazy female, he told himself. But another voice inside him refused to let him wheel the Ovaro around. She hadn't been frightened enough to flee. She was too hard-nosed for that, he had already learned. And she hadn't been wandering the mesa lost. She had left her horse safely out of sight to climb onto the rocks and spy on the six Apache, much as he had done himself. She had a reason for spying, just as she now had a reason for running. Damn, Fargo swore softly as he put the Ovaro into a trot. He was going to find out the answers.

Maybe he was wasting his time, he realized, but maybe, just maybe, the beautiful blond might give him something to report back to Tom Carpenter. He sure as hell hadn't anything else to report and it was time to head back to the army command post in Adobles. Fargo rode alongside the tracks in the soil and saw the girl had held her big gray to a gallop until the horse began to shorten stride. The tracks told him she had then brought him back to a canter and soon into a walk as the fast-rising heat of the day drained the energies of horse and rider.

Fargo slowed, a tight smile touching his lips as he reached a cluster of mesquite trees. She had turned at the trees and sent her horse along a trail of older hoofprints, but the tracks of the big, heavy-footed gray were unmistakable.

Fargo followed patiently and the low foothills of the mountains rose up as the soil grew harder, firmer. She had skirted the first rise of land and headed between two low hills where a passageway opened. Fargo halted the Ovaro as he reached the start of the passageway, edged the horse to the right side of the pass, and pulled himself from the saddle onto an outcrop of rock. He rested a moment, secured his footing, and climbed up onto the flat top of the outcrop to lie on his stomach. He peered down to where the end of the passage opened onto a small circle between the two foothills, and spotted the girl at once, her gold-wheat hair catching the sun so that it looked like yellow flame.

She was seated against a rock, taking small sips from a canteen as she chewed on a piece of hardtack. She was even more attractive relaxed, he noted, the hardness gone from the very blue eyes, the line of her face softened. She'd opened the top buttons of the gray shirt and he saw the lovely swell of one breast as she leaned on her elbow. Fargo, staying on his stomach, inched his way along the flat rock until he was closer to her. He paused as she rose, her eyes casting a quick glance along the hills but passing over where he lay on the rock. She'd put the big gray in the shade of a tall slab of rock, and as she put the rest of the hardtack into her saddlebag, Fargo pushed himself to his feet. He half-turned as he leapt from the rock and landed almost in front of her on the balls of his feet.

She spun around, a frown of surprise digging into her smooth brow.

"I don't like to be stood up," Fargo growled.

The girl's very blue eyes darkened as she recovered from her initial surprise, and he saw the hardness come into her face. "You do have clothes," she commented tartly.

Fargo fixed her with a hard stare. "I didn't track you down so you could be smart-ass," he said. "Why'd you light out?"

She shrugged. "Thought maybe it was best."

He let the answer go. "Talk," he grunted. "You've a name. Start with that."

"Blossom Daley," she said, meeting the hardness of his gaze with a steady stare. "What else?"

"Same question. Why were you watching those Apache from the rocks?" Fargo said.

"I was hiding from them," Blossom Daley said.

Fargo made a wry face. "Try again, Blossom, honey," he said.

Her lips tightened. "That's my answer. Why were *you* there?" she tossed back.

"Waiting to get a closer look at them, but you blew it all apart," Fargo growled.

A frown of consternation passed over her attractive

24

face. "I don't know why they suddenly knew I was there. I hadn't made a sound," she said.

"They picked up that damn perfume you're wearing," Fargo snapped.

"Cologne," she cut in.

"Whatever it is, the wind carried it right to them. That's why I was all but naked. Any Apache is like a prairie wolf. What he doesn't see or hear, he can usually smell. I knew they'd pick up the scent of leather and wool carrying white man's sweat after a long day's ride," he told her.

She nodded, and he saw the new respect come into the very blue eyes that stared back at him. "You do this often?" Blossom asked.

"Often enough," he said.

"Who are you?" Blossom asked with a frown.

"Name's Fargo, Skye Fargo. Some call me the Trailsman," he told her.

The blue eyes continued to study him. "Why did you want a closer look at those Apache?" she asked.

"Wanted to see what tribe they were," he answered.

"Why?" Blossom pressed, and Fargo realized with a surge of anger that she had deftly turned the questioning around. She hadn't just been hiding from the six Apache, he grunted silently. He was all but certain of that, and he decided to prove his thoughts. He kept his voice casual as he answered.

"Been looking for the Apache that grabbed a man named Dale Talbot," he said, and saw the surprise flash momentarily in the very blue eyes. She recovered quickly but not before her lips also tightened for an instant. "Know anything about him?" he slid at her mildly.

"No, nothing," Blossom answered too quickly, and Fargo kept the smile inside himself.

"Just wondered." He smiled affably. "Now, you

25

want to tell me why you were watching those Apache?"

"I did. I told you I was hiding from them," she said.

"Bullshit, honey," he said pleasantly, seeing anger leap into her eyes.

"You've no cause to say that," she snapped back. "I lost my way when night came. I spotted them and hid in the rocks."

"Lost your way from what, honey?" Fargo questioned.

She almost stammered but controlled herself. "From looking for some friends who went out this way in a wagon," Blossom said.

"What kind of wagon?" Fargo stabbed at her.

"I don't know. I'm no expert on wagons," she flung back.

"Whatever you say, Blossom, honey," Fargo commented, and his smile of patient disbelief drew a glower from her. He whistled sharply through his teeth and the Ovaro at once trotted through the passage between the rocks. "I'll be riding back," he said as he pulled himself onto the horse. "You going to keep wandering around lost?"

"I'm not lost anymore, now that it's day," she said, and walked to the sturdy gray.

"Good," he said to her, noting again the extra, full pack on her horse.

Blossom paused beside her horse and he saw her face soften as her eyes found him. She was a a damn attractive female, he noted again, his glance lingering on the soft, round curves of her breasts under the gray shirt. "I owe you," she said. "Can't do more than say thanks now. Maybe another time and another place I can repay you."

"Maybe," he agreed. "Don't get lost again." He smiled as he turned the Ovaro and trotted back through the passage, reached the top of the small

26

slope, and halted to watch Blossom walk the big gray down the other side of the hill. She had lied about why she'd watched the Apache, and Dale Talbot's name had meant something to her, Fargo thought, but that didn't explain why she was wandering around out here by her very lovely self. The Apache had shaken her some, but she still plainly thought she could handle whatever came along.

He made a wry face. She was quick, sharp, and hard-nosed, but she was also fooling herself. Maybe Tom Carpenter, could supply some information about Blossom Daley, Fargo mused as he moved the Ovaro north and started back toward Rio Hondo. In any case, he had the very definite feeling he hadn't seen the last of Blossom Daley's blond loveliness. Unless she went and got herself caught by the Apache again, he thought. He hoped she'd learned from the night's lesson and washed off her cologne. He was almost tempted to trail her some more, but he was expected back at the command post and he sent the Ovaro into a trot.

He hadn't gone more than a quarter of a mile when he glimpsed the three horsemen riding northwest, and he steered the Ovaro behind a sandstone pinnacle as they approached. They passed only a dozen yards from him, heading in the direction Blossom had gone on the gray. Fargo's eyes peered at the three men as they passed and his mouth tightened. Desert rats, he guessed. Cracked, worn leather, shabby clothes, broken cinch rings, gave them away, but mostly their faces told what they were. They had the mean-eyed hound-dog look of those used to scrounging their way through the world. The one in the lead wore a heavy stubble around his jaw, the second one sported a stained stetson, while the third was distinguished by the bandanna around his head.

Fargo stayed behind the pinnacle as the trio rode up

the side of the slope and halted. He saw the stubble-faced one point to the ground. They had seemed to be following Blossom's tracks, and he watched them quickly change direction to follow the trail. A lone set of prints meant an easy mark. Damn, Fargo swore. They'd pounce on Blossom the way a weasel would pounce on a prairie chicken.

The three riders vanished from view as Fargo frowned. The major had paid him to bring back something to report on Dale Talbot, and he'd nothing but Blossom Daley. Besides, she was too damn good-looking to leave to the likes of those three desert rats. With a soft oath, he swung the Ovaro around and sent the horse up into the rock formations that dotted the foothills.

He rode along the top of a low hill until the three horsemen came into sight again, and he dropped the Ovaro down to move along the far slope of the hill where he could watch them and stay out of sight. They were riding hard now, hurrying after the single set of hoofprints, and as he watched, Blossom came into view, riding slowly down to the base of the low hill. He saw her as she heard the approaching riders and turned in the saddle to glance back.

As he expected, she didn't try to run when she saw that the horsemen approaching were not Apache and Fargo moved forward closer as the three men caught up to her. Blossom halted and the trio formed a half-circle around her. He was too far away to hear, but he saw Blossom quickly realize that the three men wanted only one thing. She yanked the gray around to run, but the one with the bandanna leapt from his horse and grabbed the gray's bridle. He saw the stained stetson move in and reach out to grab her around the waist, and Blossom's arm lashed out, a rid-ing crop in her hand. He heard the man scream in pain as the crop whipped across his face. Blossom tried to bring the crop around again, but the stubble-faced one came up from behind and pushed with both hands. Fargo saw Blossom fall from the saddle and land on her hands and knees.

The stained stetson was atop her instantly, and Fargo sent the Ovaro over the top of the low hill at a fast canter as the man wrestled Blossom onto her back. "Goddamn bitch, you'll pay for that," Fargo heard him shout as he backhanded Blossom across the face. He straddled the girl as she lay on her back, slapping her twice. Fargo saw Blossom's thick blond head swing from side to side with the force of the blows.

The stubble-faced man and the other one had dismounted and were at Blossom's legs, throwing her skirt up, and Fargo glimpsed shapely calves below pink bloomers as she tried to kick out. But one held her legs as the other started to rip the pink bloomers down. They were intent on their work and turned to look up only as Fargo galloped to a halt. The one in the stained stetson stayed atop Blossom and continued to slap her across the face.

"Fun's over," Fargo said as he reined to a halt, one hand on the butt of his holstered Colt.

The other two rose to their feet, frowns on their mean-eyed faces as they peered at the big man on the Ovaro. The stained stetson stopped slapping Blossom to look up at the intruder from where he sat atop her, and Fargo saw a thin line of red across his face. "Who're you?" the man rasped.

"Doesn't matter. Let her up," Fargo said, and saw Blossom's eyes staring at him, fear and fury mixed in their blue depths.

The man's face twisted with a sneer of contempt. "Kill the stupid shit," he barked at the other two.

Fargo saw the two men start to reach for their guns. "I wouldn't follow those orders," he said.

The two men hesitated for a fraction of a second.

"Kill him, goddammit," the stained stetson barked.

The two men's hands went into motion again and Fargo almost sighed as he snapped the big Colt from its holster with a motion as quick as a diamondback's strike. The two shots sounded almost as one and both men twisted, staggered, and fell as though they had been toppled by the same invisible rope.

"Should've listened to me," Fargo muttered as his eyes fastened on the stained stetson. The man still straddled Blossom but his face was turned to the big man atop the Ovaro. "Get up," Fargo growled. "Slow and easy." The man obeyed, pushing himself up from Blossom, who scooted backward and got to her feet. Fargo saw her leg flash up and out, the kick hitting the man full in the groin.

"Ow, Jesus," the man gasped as he clutched at himself and fell to his knees in pain.

"Bastard," Blossom hissed. She swung a right that smashed the man across the face as he continued to clutch his groin.

"That's enough," Fargo said, and Blossom halted another kick she had begun to aim at him. "You don't want to do that," he chided.

"The hell I don't," Blossom snapped, glaring.

"Damn but you're a little hard-nose," Fargo commented. "Back off." Blossom obeyed but the glare stayed in her face and Fargo's eyes flicked to the stained stetson. The man was still bent over on his knees, his left hand still pressing his groin, his face averted. His right arm was hidden from Fargo's view, but he caught the faint movement of the man's shoulder and raised the big Colt instantly. The gun was aimed as the man brought his arm around with the six-gun in his hand. Fargo fired and the stetson took on a new stain of dark red as it blew apart. He saw Blossom turn her face away and wince as the almost headless figure fell onto its back. "You pay for being stupid,"

Fargo said. He holstered the big Colt and saw Blossom's blue eyes return to him. "You're becoming a real pain in the ass, honey," he remarked.

"You followed me," Blossom said.

"No. I saw them head after you," Fargo answered.

"That makes two I owe," she said.

"I don't figure to make it three," Fargo told her harshly, and saw the hint of a pout touch her pretty face. "You're fair game for anything out here and you don't want to admit it."

"I've things to do," she said.

"You'd best ride back to Adobles with me," Fargo said and watched her pause in thought.

"Maybe I should," she said. "But not because I can't take care of myself," she added hastily.

"You could've fooled me," he grunted.

"I was taken by surprise, both times," Blossom said.

"That's pretty much how everything happens out here," he said.

"It won't happen again," Blossom said firmly. "But I will go back with you. I don't want to seem ungrateful."

"That's nice," Fargo responded dryly. She was as quick with an answer as she was hard-nosed, he thought, and waited as she pulled herself up onto the gray. "Now, you want to tell me what you're doing out here while we ride," he said as he turned the Ovaro northward.

"I told you. Don't you ever believe anybody?" Blossom said.

"Sometimes. This isn't one of them," Fargo's casual reply drew a sharp glance from her. "Where are you from?" he questioned.

"Does it matter?" she answered.

"It might. Besides, I just like knowing those things. Maybe I should tell you," he said, and her brows lifted a fraction.

"Go ahead," she said.

He pursed his lips as he studied her for a long moment. "Someplace northeast of Kentucky," he said. "Or just down into the Kentucky land." He laughed as her mouth fell open in surprise.

"What makes you say that?" she said, trying to recover.

"You dress well enough to be a New Orleans gal, but you don't have the New Orleans talk in you," he said.

"That all?"

"No. That big gray of yours. You don't find that kind of horse in these parts. You don't find it up in the Plains territories, either. That's an eastern horse, standardbred in him. You've got eastern riding boots to go with him," Fargo said.

"Anything else?" she said tartly, but there was deepened respect in the blue eyes.

He chuckled. "You think being hard-nosed will see you through out here. Anybody lives out here knows better," he said, and saw her mouth tighten for an instant.

"You are good, aren't you?" Blossom said, and he shrugged. "I'm from Virginia," she added.

"Rubs shoulders with Washington, doesn't it?" Fargo commented, and she nodded. "I still want to know what you're doing out here."

"Let's say personal business," Blossom answered.

"You owe me more than that, honey," Fargo said.

Blossom's lips thinned and she looked uncomfortable for an instant. "Maybe, when it's time," she said stubbornly.

Fargo nodded, deciding to let her play her little game out, whatever it was.

The night began to slide across the hot ground and he found a spot to make camp between two sandstone pinnacles. He found enough dry brush for a small fire to warm the beef jerky and then let the fire burn itself out as the moon rose to turn the arid land a dull silver.

Blossom gathered her things and stepped into a crack in the pinnacle to change. She returned in a black robe with red facing, the neckline deep enough to let him see the rise of her breasts. She halted before him, her eyes searching his face. "I know you're thinking I ought to do something about being grateful," Blossom muttered.

"You're half right," Fargo said.

"What's that mean?" Blossom asked.

"It means being grateful isn't the only reason for doing things. Just wanting to is enough," he answered.

She looked away, her brow creasing in a tiny furrow of thought. It stayed as she returned her eyes to him. "I don't know enough about you yet," Blossom said gravely.

"Ask," Fargo said.

"No. I'll find out my own way," she said, and he smiled.

"Too bad." He shrugged, and Blossom took a step toward him, lifting her arms to encircle his neck. Her lips were warm and soft, and he felt the faint pressure of her breasts under the robe. She pulled away when he opened his lips to respond. "What was that for?" he asked.

"To show I'm grateful and to ask for more time," Blossom said.

He half-shrugged and watched her move away to slip under the blanket she had laid out. He returned to his bedroll, undressed to his B.V.D.s, and stretched his muscled, magnificent physicque, feeling Blossom's eyes watching him. He stretched again and lay down on his bedroll as Blossom flounced onto her side, her back to him, and he heard the anger in her movement. "Sleep well," he said.

"You did that on purpose," she muttered from under the blanket.

"Don't know what you mean," he said innocently.

"Hell, you don't," she muttered again. "Good night."

He chuckled as he closed his eyes and let sleep sweep over him.

The night was still and he slept without interruption until he woke, the sun growing hot even as he pulled on clothes. Blossom sat up, her hair a cascade of yellow around her face, and he saw to the horses as she disappeared into the rocks to dress. She emerged looking surprisingly fresh and prettier than ever in a dark-green shirt and matching riding skirt. As she gathered her things together, Fargo walked to where he had spotted a large cluster of dried chia, and holding his palm cupped and outstretched, he knocked a handful of the little brown-and-white chia seeds from the bushes. Blossom was on the big gray when he returned, and he poured half the little seeds into her hand. "Breakfast," he said as she stared down at her palm.

"These little seeds?" she frowned.

"A teaspoon of chia seeds can keep an Apache going for a full day," he said. "The Indians use them in all kinds of ways for all kinds of things. They're full of damn near everything you need." He swung onto the Ovaro and led the way north, munching on the chia seeds slowly as he rode with Blossom beside him. His eyes continued to sweep the dry countryside as they traveled, but the land stayed quiet and he let himself enjoy Blossom's blond loveliness. She rode with her back held straight and the modest breasts swayed gently under the dark-green shirt.

"How much farther?" she asked as the sun began to climb into the noonday sky.

"Another hour or two, I'd guess," he answered.

He caught the quick little glance she shot at him before she voiced the next question. "This man you're looking for, Dale Talbot, you know anything about him?" she asked with a good try at keeping her voice casual.

"Only that his brother's a senator in Washington," Fargo returned with equal offhandedness.

"Why are you looking for him?" Blossom asked, still working hard at keeping her questions idly casual.

"Major Carpenter paid me to try to get him some leads," Fargo said. "Tom Carpenter's an old friend as well as commander of the Forty-first Cavalry out here."

"That's all? Just the major?" Blossom pressed, and lost some of the casualness in her voice. "Nobody else pay you to look?"

"Nobody else," he said. "Why?"

"Just curious," she said, and cast him another quick glance, but he kept his handsome face impassive. She lapsed into silence, and as they rode over a low hill, Adobles came into sight.

The town consisted of mostly Mexican-style squat, flat-roofed buildings. The cavalry command post, a cluster of army barracks, adjoined the entrance to the town.

Fargo rode with Blossom to the town's single boardinghouse, one of the few frame buildings in Adobles, and he waited as she dismounted and went inside. When she emerged, she carried a key ring with a single large key on it in one hand, and he dismounted as she took the big gray to the stable two doors from the boardinghouse. He was leaning against the doorpost of the house when she returned, blond hair glistening in the high sun.

"How long do you plan to stay?" he asked.

"Depends," she said carefully, and he smiled inside himself. Her caution was almost amusing, and he couldn't bring himself to shatter her little game. "Why you asking?" she tossed at him.

"Maybe I'll come visit," he answered.

"Don't be expecting," she muttered.

"Don't be wishing," he laughed, and saw her eyes flare.

He turned and swung onto the Ovaro. She watched him as he rode across the main street of the town and up to the cluster of army buildings. He halted and dismounted outside the building with the red-and-black pennant flying from a rooftop pole. He went inside and found the door to Tom Carpenter's office open. He strode in only to halt in surprise. The face that looked up at him from behind the desk was neither lined, nor long and drawn, nor topped with graying hair and captain's bars adorned the collar of the blue uniform. The face was so young, it was almost pink-cheeked, made of small, neat features under sandy-colored hair carefully combed. The captain tried to let an air of condescension give him authority. It probably succeeded with some people, Fargo mused, but to him it seemed simply ridiculous.

"Sorry, I expected Major Carpenter," Fargo said.

"He's left," the young officer said crisply.

"Left?" Fargo echoed.

"Gone back to Kansas, family emergency. I'm commanding the Forty-first in his place," the officer said, keeping his words firm and crisp.

"You?" Fargo frowned, aware that a combination of astonishment and disbelief had crossed his face.

"Yes. Captain Ambrose Ellwood," the officer said, and rose to his feet to add dignity to his announcement. He seemed short next to the big man with the stabbing lake-blue eyes.

"Skye Fargo," the Trailsman said, and saw the captain's eyes widen.

"You're the man Major Carpenter hired." he said.

"The one they call the Trailsman." Fargo nodded and the younger man reached into a desk drawer and pulled out an envelope. "The major left this for you."

Fargo took the envelope and saw his name written neatly across it. Beside his name, in large letters, was the word PERSONAL.

Capt. Ellwood's voice cut into his thoughts as he stared down at the envelope. "I'm glad you're here, Fargo," the captain said, unable to keep the tinge of officiousness out of his voice, Fargo noted. "Senator Talbot is in Adobles. I've scheduled a meeting here for the morning, but I want to hear what you have to report now."

"Maybe I'd better read this first," Fargo said as he eased himself onto a straight-backed chair and opened the envelope.

Fargo, old friend,

Sorry I had to run out on you. Sickness in the family. You've met Captain Ellwood if you're reading this. I'm even less happy than you are at what the big brass sent to take over while I'm gone. I've long stopped trying to understand their thinking.

Don't know how long I'll be gone, maybe weeks, maybe months, but I'm asking you to follow through on this as if I were there. God knows Ellwood is going to need help and you've been paid and are technically under contract to the army, though I know neither of us gives a tinker's damn about that. I don't know what this is all about, and if there is a man that can still be rescued alive from the Apache, I think he deserves our effort to save him.

So that leaves only you, Fargo. Give it what you can for me. Hope I'll see you again soon.

Tom Carpenter,
Major, United States Cavalry

Thoughtfully, Fargo folded the letter in half and slowly tore it into little pieces, aware that Capt.

37

Ambrose Ellwood watched him. "That personal?" the captain asked.

"Yep," Fargo said, and dropped the torn pieces into a spittoon just outside the doorway of the office. He leaned back and surveyed the unlined face of the young officer, and the question refused to stay on the back of his tongue. "Why you?" he asked, and saw the captain's smooth brow furrow. "Why'd they pick you to send out here?"

"I did an extensive study of this area when I was at the military academy—its history, its people, and especially the Indians," the captain said.

"Where were you before they sent you out here?" Fargo probed.

"General staff headquarters," the captain said.

"Desk work. Shit," Fargo grunted.

The captain drew himself up stiffly. "I graduated with highest honors at the academy and I'm considered an expert on the Southwest territories," he said.

"An expert out of books. Jesus," Fargo said.

"I assure you, I know everything about this territory," the captain said.

"You don't know a woman because you've got a picture of one, and you don't know the Indian out of a book," Fargo said. "Truth is, Captain, you don't know shit about this territory."

"You're entitled to your opinions, Fargo," Capt. Ellwood said icily. "However, I'm in charge here and I'm completely confident of my knowledge. I want you to be at the meeting with Senator Talbot tomorrow. It'll show the senator we've tried to do something."

"If I'm back in time," Fargo said.

"Where are you going?" The young officer frowned.

"Look up an old contact. Might help us," Fargo said.

"See that you're back in time for the meeting," the captain said.

Fargo rose, flattened both palms on the desk, and leaned forward until his face was but inches from the captain's unlined cheeks. "I'll be back when I'm back," he said, his voice hard steel.

Capt. Ambrose Ellwood swallowed hard. "Major Carpenter told me you could be difficult to handle," he said.

"I'm not difficult. You've just got to learn who not to give orders to," Fargo said, straightening up and walking out of the office as the captain swallowed again.

Outside, Fargo found that dusk had lowered a purple veil across the dry land, and he mounted the Ovaro and rode from the army post. He slowed outside the boardinghouse, but decided to put off visiting Blossom. He'd something more important to do, and he headed the horse east as a half-moon began to creep along the new night sky. A red wolf howled in the distance as he rode across the flatland and the night cooled the hot, sandy soil.

The town lay about an hour north of Adobles. It had a name, Roca Blanca, but it was really a handful of Mexican-style buildings clustered around a saloon. He hadn't been there in years, but as it came into sight, he saw that nothing had changed. He reined up outside the saloon where a square of yellow light streamed out into the night. He dismounted and entered the square room. The ornate crystal chandelier seemed totally out of place above the rough-hewn wooden tables and the old, splintered bar. His eyes moved slowly over the men at the bar, turned to scan the tables that took up most of the room. He searched for a weathered face that carried at least threescore and ten years but with hair still black as coal on a long, narrow frame not unlike a knobby length of basswood. But no such face met his gaze and he saw the woman came toward him, overblown, overrouged, brass-gold hair, big breasts held in shape by a red dress two sizes too small.

"Hello, big feller." She smiled. "You're new here."

"Looking for Yuma Kelly," Fargo said. "Figured he'd be here by now."

"You a friend of his?" the woman asked cautiously.

"From way back," Fargo said.

"Then you'd best go after him quick, or you'll find him shot full of holes," she said. "He just lit out of here with three big varmints after him."

"Why?" Fargo frowned.

"He was playing seven-card stud with these three when he caught them cheating," she said. "The old fool, all he had to do was fold and quit the game. But if you know Yuma Kelly, you know what he did."

"He called them on it," Fargo said.

"Yep, and he's too old to call out three gun-toting card cheats. They went for him. The bartender tossed a chair in their way and it gave Yuma a chance to get outside, but they went hot after him," the woman said.

"Goddamn. I need him alive and in one piece," Fargo swore as he spun and raced out of the saloon. He hit the saddle with a flying leap and the Ovaro raced off at once as he bent low and picked up the tracks of the three horses, hoofmarks dug deep into the dry ground as they gave chase. He put the Ovaro into a full gallop as he followed the tracks and saw that Yuma had headed for the little pueblo-style house where he lived north of the town where the Rio Hondo met the Pecos.

Fargo heard the sound of gunfire as he raced across the first low hill and he slowed the horse as he came in sight of the lone, flat-roofed house that rested in a small dip of land between two low hills heavily grown with brush and a half-dozen shriveled black locust trees. The gunfire sounded again and Fargo saw that

Yuma Kelly had holed up inside his house, his attackers spread out in the dry brush. Fargo guided the Ovaro up the far side of the hill, halted, and swung to the ground to make his way down the other side of the hill on foot.

He headed toward the rear of Yuma's little house and paused, his eyes straining down the hillside in the moonlight. He heard one of the men call out, a high, nasal voice with a nasty whine in it. "You ain't comin' out alive, old man," the voice said.

"Come in and get me, you card-cheatin' bastards," Fargo heard Yuma shout back. He stayed motionless on the hillside for a moment longer and then slowly slid down through the brush until he had made a half-circle to the rear of the house. He paused again as a flurry of shots erupted to chip away pieces of the house's soft stone and thud into the wooden door. Fargo saw a figure dart in a crouch through the brush and sink down opposite the right side of the house. The flurry of shots had been only to make Yuma stay down while the figure darted to the side of the house, Fargo saw, and he watched the man begin to inch his way down toward the side window of the little house. The other two figures fired again and this time drew an answering round from Yuma.

Fargo's eyes stayed on the man that edged down through the brush toward the side window of the house. Yuma was plainly hunkered down at the front window, which let him cover the approach to the door. It was just as obvious that he was completely unaware of the figure creeping down the hill to the side window of the house.

Fargo rose to a crouch and moved down the hill as he unholstered the big Colt. The figure almost in front of him had paused, a six-gun in hand, only a few feet from the side window. He was waiting for something, Fargo realized, and the answer exploded in another furious volley of shots aimed at the front door and window of the house. The figure rose and started to race the few yards to the side window as the fusillade thundered. Fargo raised the Colt, took quick aim, and fired, his single shot blending in with the sound of the other shots. He saw the figure pitching forward to lay still just at the edge of the last of the brush.

The volley of shots ended and Fargo dropped to one knee. He could see the other two men where they crouched in the brush, their gaze focused on the little house. They waited for the sound of their partner sending a hail of bullets into Yuma from the side window. But there was no flurry of shots, and though they were too far away for him to see details, Fargo knew they were frowning by now. Their consternation was growing and he knew they'd exchanged tense whispers. He smiled and stayed motionless. It took only a few minutes for the two figures to give in to alarm and curiosity, and he saw one begin to work himself sideways across the hillside as the other fired a few desultory shots at the house.

Fargo dropped low in the brush and watched the man crawl across the hillside until he reached a spot that faced the side of Yuma's house. He began to slide slowly downward, much as the first one had done, and Fargo lay in wait as the man passed him. The man had neared the bottom of the hill when he came to an abrupt halt, and Fargo heard his sharp gasp of astonishment as he saw the body stretched out at the edge of the brush. Fargo lifted himself to one knee and raised the Colt.

"Got himself shot," he said in a whisper just loud enough for the man to hear. The man's head snapped up and he whirled, gun in hand. Fargo dropped as the gun exploded, a sweep of bullets into the brush, all too high and too wide. Fargo's single shot blended into the volley and the man toppled backward, rolled, and came to a stop only a foot away from the first figure.

Silence followed, and Fargo rose up onto one elbow to peer over at the third figure crouched in the brush on the front of the hill. He let the silence become an unnerving, soundless blanket. Hardly a minute had gone past when he heard the nasal whine call out.

"Sowey? You there? Eddie?" the man called. "Answer me, dammit? You get him?" Fargo watched as the man grew still and listened. But he heard only the silence. "What the hell's goin' on? Eddie, you hear me?" he called out again, and Fargo heard the note of alarm come into his voice. But it was Yuma who answered from inside the house.

"Stop wastin' your breath. You're not trickin' me into comin' out there," Yuma called.

Fargo's eyes stayed on the figure halfway up the hill. The man knew he wasn't playing tricks, and his senses told him something had gone very wrong. Sudden fear did the rest, and Fargo watched him begin to scoot backward up the hill. When he neared the top, he rose and began to run toward where the horses waited. Fargo watched as the man hit the saddle and vanished over the top of the low hill, hoofbeats quickly fading away as the horse raced into the night. Fargo rose to his feet as he called out. "You can come out, now, you old goat."

He waited in the silence that followed and then Yuma's voice lifted, filled with surprise and caution. "Who's that?" the old man called.

"Somebody who just saved your worthless old carcass," Fargo answered, and he could almost see Yuma's frown of consternation.

"Fargo?" Yuma called back after a moment. "Is that you, Fargo?"

"It's me," the Trailsman said.

Yuma's head carefully poked up over the top of the

windowsill, and Fargo straightened up. "I'll be dammed. It *is* you," Yuma Kelly exploded.

"In the flesh," Fargo agreed, and saw Yuma jump to his feet and run to the door. He came out, long legs flying, his gun still in hand.

"What happened to those three varmints?" Yuma frowned.

"One hightailed it. I got the other two when they were going to blast you from the side window," Fargo said.

"I'll be dammed. Never heard you out here at all," Yuma Kelly said.

"Neither did they. I used their fire as cover," Fargo said.

"Well, you picked the right time to come calling," Yuma said as he holstered his gun.

"Saloon gal in Roca Banca told me what happened," Fargo said. "You're still doing boneheaded things, I see."

Yuma Kelly's weathered face managed to look almost sheepish. "You know me, Fargo. I hate card-cheatin' varmints," he said. "But, Jesus, it's good to see you. Come on in. I've some good bourbon."

"Now, that sounds inviting," Fargo said, and followed Yuma Kelly into the small, square house. He perched on a serape-covered wooden chest as Yuma fetched the whiskey and two shot glasses. Yuma hadn't changed any, Fargo saw, the old man's tall, spare frame still hard as a length of basswood, the eyes that peered out of his parchment face still bright and alert.

"Obliged," Yuma said as he lifted his shot glass in salute. "But you didn't come all the way out here into New Mexico just to visit with me."

Fargo's laugh conceded the remark, and he told of the summons from Major Carpenter. When he finished, Yuma Kelly's weathered face had taken on added wrinkles of distaste. "I heard about the Apache taking a white man," he said.

"You hear it from that guide who hid out and saved his skin?" Fargo asked.

"Johnny Kelter," Yuma said. "Yes, I know him."

"He see anything that'd help?"

"Hell, no, he was too scared to look," Yuma said. "Johnny Kelter's not much of anything to begin with."

"He mention where this Dale Talbot was headed?" Fargo asked.

"To Mexico, I heard," Yuma said.

Fargo took in the one, lone fact that had come his way so far. "Meet me at the army post in Adobles tomorrow morning. There's a meeting set up by the new captain in charge."

"What happened to the Major?"

"Called back on a family crisis," Fargo said.

"I'll be there." Yuma nodded as he finished his bourbon, rose, took a shovel from a corner, and handed Fargo another. "Give me a hand getting rid of those two sidewinders. They don't deserve buryin', but I don't want the buzzards hanging around here all week," he said.

"Let's get at it," Fargo said, and drained the shot glass. The bourbon felt warm as it made its way through him. "Where'd you get such good whiskey?" he asked, and Yuma laughed.

"Half my pay for a job," Yuma said. "What're you offering?"

"You just got paid in advance," Fargo told him.

"Guess so," Yuma grunted.

Fargo followed Yuma from the house and helped dispose of the two men some hundred yards back of the hill. The ground was dry and easy to dig, and he was riding back toward Adobles before an hour had passed. He headed southwest, skirted Roca Blanca, and found Adobles a still, dark place when he reached

45

it. He halted at the boardinghouse, dismounted, and entered. The clerk inside pulled his eyes open to peer at him. "Blossom Daley," Fargo said.

"Room four, end of the hall," the man said.

Fargo went down the dim hallway and saw the edge of lamplight at the bottom of the door. He knocked softly and she took a moment to answer, opening the door cautiously. She wore a light-blue floor-length nightdress, he saw, with a lace edge at the neckline that showed the swell of her breasts. "Kind of late to come calling," Blossom said.

"Been busy," Fargo said. He kept his voice casual, but he had prepared his words. "Tried to get a lead on this Dale Talbot," he said.

"Oh?" Blossom said, and opened the door wider at once. "Find out anything?" she asked as he stepped into the room.

"No, and I've a meeting tomorrow with the new captain in charge here and Senator Robert Talbot," Fargo said.

"He's here? In Adobles?" Blossom asked, her very blue eyes growing wide.

"Got in yesterday, I was told," Fargo said.

"Is he alone?" Blossom asked.

Fargo shrugged. "Don't know. For somebody who's just curious, you seem awfully interested, Blossom, honey," he commented.

She kept her face composed, but he caught the flicker in her eyes. "Any law against being curious?" she said.

"Guess not." Fargo smiled as he reached out and curled one arm around the back of her waist. He pulled her to him and his mouth pressed down on her lips and he tasted their sweet warmth. He pressed harder and felt her lips give a fraction. His hand rose to stroke the side of her face, down along her neck, and moved down to caress her shoulder, edged to the top soft curve of one breast. She gave a tiny gasp at his touch and he felt her hand tighten against his chest. He let his thumb rub gently across the top of the swelling line of her breast, and with a half-cry she twisted away from him. Her eyes were twin pools of turbulent blue as she glowered at him.

"No," she said between quick, hard breaths. "You'd no call to do that."

"Any law against being curious?" He smiled.

Her face set. "Guess not," she echoed, and tossed back her long, thick blond hair. He reached out again, both hands this time, closing his palms around her shoulders as he drew her to him. His mouth came down to her lips again and he felt her mouth open, hold back, then grow soft. His hands moved down from her shoulders to rub against the soft sides of her breasts. He felt her tongue slip forward across his lips, and then her hands were pushing at him as with a gasped cry she tore away from him once again. "You're more than curious," she said, glaring.

"That makes two of us," he shot back.

She set her face at once. "I don't know what you're talking about," she said stiffly.

"Still want to play games," he said wryly.

Her eyes stayed on him, studying, trying to probe through him. "Come back to see me after your meeting tomorrow," she said.

"Give me a good reason," he said.

She hesitated, and he saw thoughts racing behind the very blue eyes until she stepped closer and this time it was her mouth that sought his, her lips parting as she pressed herself against him for a brief moment that was long enough to let him feel the softness of her. She drew back, her eyes grave. "Reason enough?" she asked.

"Maybe," he allowed, and saw her watch him as he left and pulled the door shut after him. He strolled from the boardinghouse as thoughts played leapfrog in his mind. Blossom was hardly as cleverly subtle as she thought, he laughed. She continued to play her little game, whatever it was. She'd asked him back to pump him about the meeting while she'd continue to play the innocent, he was sure. But somehow, someway, Blossom was involved in Dale Talbot's capture by the Apache, and she was plainly unwilling to trust anyone but herself. He paused beside his horse outside, a frown digging into his brow. That still didn't explain what she hoped to do out here alone. It was time to find out more about Blossom Daley, he decided, and he led the Ovaro the few doors down from the boardinghouse to the stable where Blossom had put the big gray.

A stableman appeared, his watery, rheumy eyes appraising Fargo, a bridle held in one hand. "Miss Daley's horse," Fargo said. "Big gray. She wants me to give him a fast curry."

The stableman frowned. "Damn late hour for that," he muttered, and Fargo smelled the odor of bad whiskey on him.

"She wants him ready, come morning," he said.

The rheumy eyes held their suspicious glance. "I don't know, mister," the stableman said.

"Sure you do," he said, and tossed a gold piece he had taken from his pocket. It would buy enough whiskey for a week.

The man caught the coin as it spiraled to him. "Stable six," he said. "Saddle and gear in the back room."

Fargo walked into the dimly lighted stable, down the aisle between the stalls until he found the big gray. He put a rope halter on the horse and led it into the wide, open back area of the stable where saddles and other gear lined the walls in place under stable numbers. Aware that the stableman was most likely peering back to watch, he found a curry and began to groom the horse. He continued to give the horse a fast currying until he heard the sounds of the stableman working on the bridle in the front part of the stable. Fargo put the curry down and stepped to where the extra pack Blossom had on the horse lay beneath her saddle.

He pulled the thick pack out from under the saddle, knelt down on one knee, and untied the ropes around it. As he did, the sides of the pack fell open and he peeled the top of the pack back and stared at the contents beneath. The beads caught his eye first, dozens of strings of different-colored beads, and beneath them, perhaps two dozen combs of different shapes, sizes, and colors. Mixed in the pack of trinkets he saw hand mirrors, pocket watches, brooches, hair clips, bonnets, neatly folded lace shawls, pieces of colored glass, a half-dozen children's toys, and two harmonicas. He stared at the array of baubles and bangles and heard the small grunt that fell from his lips. The entire pack was filled with objects that could be used in dealing with the Indians. She'd done her homework well on that, he conceded. She plainly expected to trade or buy her way to something with the Apache. To information about Dale Talbot? The question asked itself and hung unanswered in his thoughts. He stared down at the pack of trinkets again and felt his lips draw back in a grimace. The pack was more than a careful collection of trinkets; it was a monument to being completely and totally naive.

He shook his head in disgust as he began to tie the pack together again. Finished, he put it back in place under the saddle, returned the big gray to its stall, and strolled from the stable. The rheumy-eyed stableman watched him as he left on the Ovaro.

Fargo headed the horse from town, found a spot to bed down, and stretched out on his bedroll. Maybe the meeting in the morning would shed some light on

Blossom Daley, he pondered. He shook aside the temptation to speculate and let sleep sweep over him as, across the flat mesa, a Mexican red wolf howled in the distance.

3

The morning sun was already hot, drying out whatever moistness the night had brought to the land as Fargo waited outside the army barracks and watched Yuma ride up on his brown quarter horse. Yuma swung from the saddle and fell into step beside the big man as Fargo headed for the officers' quarters.

Capt. Ambrose Ellwood appeared from the side of the building, his uniform neat, collar properly buttoned. "Go in and wait for me, Fargo," the captain said. "I'll be with you in a minute."

Fargo held the smile inside himself as he saw Yuma stare at the captain with more disbelief than surprise. "How long has he been shaving?" Yuma muttered as Capt. Ellwood disappeared around the other side of the building. Fargo made no reply as he led the way into the captain's office. Four chairs had been added to the room, he saw, and he eased himself down onto one. Yuma leaned against the wall beside him, and the captain appeared in a moment, his steps brisk and sharp. Capt. Ellwood went behind his desk at once and speared Yuma with a frown.

"Yuma Kelly," Fargo introduced. "Brought him along for the meeting."

"Why?" The captain frowned.

"Because he knows more about the Apache than any white man in the territory," Fargo said.

The captain's smile was condescending. "That may

51

be, but this is a closed meeting called by Senator Talbot," he said.

"Fine with me, sonny," Yuma said, and started to push away from the wall.

Fargo grasped his arm at once. "He goes, I go," the big man said.

"You are under contract to help in this matter, Fargo," the captain said stiffly. "Major Carpenter paid you out of army funds."

"Yuma Kelly's under contract to me," Fargo said.

"That's right, sonny," Yuma added, and received an icy glance from the captain.

"I don't know what regulations say about that," Capt. Ellwood said to Fargo.

"You go look it up. Just come back with the right answer," Fargo growled, and the captain licked his lips.

"I'll go along with you for now," he said.

"Good thinking, sonny," Yuma said.

"The captain glared at Fargo. "Tell him to stop calling me sonny," he exploded.

"I call most folks that," Yuma said. "No need to go getting all upset about it."

The captain turned angry eyes on him. "You don't call him that," he snapped, gesturing to Fargo.

"He's not wet behind the ears," Yuma said.

The captain's angry answer was cut off by the corporal who appeared in the doorway.

"Senator Talbot, sir," the soldier announced as the senator strode into the room with an air of authority that held despite his outfit of riding britches and gray frock coat. A woman came in with him, tall, clothed in a dark-gray riding outfit tailored to fit an hourglass figure.

Fargo took in the senator with one quick glance, the air of pompousness, the pepper-and-salt hair, the round face that might have been soft were it not for the hardness around his mouth, and the bright sharpness of his eyes. Fargo's glance returned to the woman. In her early thirties, he guessed, she had a small waist that rose up to large breasts, brown eyes evenly spaced in an attractive face with full red lips, a straight nose that flared slightly at the nostrils, and brown hair pulled back and held by a ribbon. She was a thoroughly handsome woman, with an air of sensuousness under the tailored severity of her outfit. He saw her eyes take him in, linger on the chiseled handsomeness of his face and the breadth of his powerful frame. She had to wrench her eyes from his as the senator introduced her to Capt. Ellwood.

"My niece, Olive Reamer," the senator said.

"My pleasure, ma'am," the captain answered. "I didn't expect a woman to be along."

"My niece has come because she was very close to my brother. We are all terribly distraught at the thought of Dale in the hands of the Apache," the senator said, and flicked a glance at the big man with the lake-blue eyes.

"This is Skye Fargo, Senator, and Yuma Kelly," the captain said. The senator's nod was curt, but Fargo saw his sharp eyes take in Yuma and himself with quick appraisal. "Fargo's widely regarded as an expert trailsman. Major Carpenter hired him to help find your brother," the captain explained. "According to Fargo, Mister Kelly is an expert on the Apache." The captain was unable to keep the condescension out of his voice.

"I do hope you can help us," the woman said, her eyes on Fargo.

"Hard truth is that he could be long dead by now," Fargo said.

"I'm aware of that," the senator said. "But we must find out. We must know, one way or the other."

Fargo shrugged and glanced past the senator's

slightly portly shape as the corporal appeared in the doorway again. "Two men here to see you, Captain," the soldier said. "About Dale Talbot, they say."

"Send them in," the captain said as a frown touched his forehead.

The two men entered the room at once, both wearing bowlers above faces that seemed very much alike. Both had thin lips and noses, and their cold eyes scanned the room at once. One, taller than the other, wore a brown tweed jacket over riding trousers, the other with a gray tweed jacket.

"Jim Robertson, Captain," the taller one said. "This is Frank Downs. We're here from the First Virginia Bank." He drew an envelope from an inside pocket and handed it to the captain. "Our credentials, Captain. You'll find them in order," he said.

"I'm sure," Capt. Ellwood said.

Fargo saw the man who'd introduced himself as Jim Robertson glance at Senator Talbot.

"Glad we got here in time," he said. "We heard the senator was coming out here to find his brother and we hurried to get here. The bank believes Dale Talbot may have had some very important bank papers with him when he fell into the hands of the Apache. We came to help try to find out what happened to him and get those papers back if we can."

"Didn't know Dale was working with the bank," the senator said tightly.

Robertson gave a thin smile. "Yes, confidential bank business," he said.

"Well, I'm sure the senator will be happy for any help in this hunt, Mister Robertson," the captain put in.

Fargo watched Senator Talbot. The senator's face showed no sign of welcoming the newcomers, his quick smile strained. In fact, he seemed decidedly unhappy at their presence.

54

Capt. Ellwood called for two more chairs to be brought in and came around to the front of his desk. "I was just about to how we might best go about finding the senator's brother," he said.

"Please go ahead," Frank Downs said as he settled himself into a chair.

"It's not a hopeless pursuit," the captain began. "I happened to have studied the history of the Apache most thoroughly."

"I'm glad to hear that," Senator Talbot said.

"Me, too," Fargo added, and saw Olive Reamer's eyes tell him that she had caught the wryness in his remark.

"Some of the Apache take slaves, so Dale Talbot could be alive," the captain said. "There are four basic tribes in the Southwest, the Jicarilla Apache, the White Mountain Apache, the Chiricahua, and the Mescalero. If we can find out which of these groups took Dale Talbot, we can know how best to deal with them."

He paused, glanced at Fargo, and saw only an expressionless attention. "The Jicarilla Apache dress most like the Plains Indians. They braid their hair and do some raising of corn, beans, and squash. The White Mountain Apache range farther west. They are more nomadic and are heavily involved in spirit worship. I'd approach the White Mountain Apaches with some sort of spiritual offering."

The captain paused again and let his eyes sweep the room to make sure he had everyone's attention. Satisfied, he went on, his voice becoming more pedagogic. "The Chiricahua are very warlike, their dwellings exclusively wickiups, most very impermanent. They tend to follow strong leaders. The last group is the Mescalero. They were never peaceful, and now they are hunters and raiders. Some say they are the fiercest of the Apache. I'd say they can best be reached through a show of force and perhaps offering them a closer look at some of our weapons. So you see, the Apache tribes are quite different from one another."

The captain halted and let his eyes circle the room with a pleased, self-satisfied expression. Fargo saw the senator digesting the captain's little lecture, Robertson and Frank Downs wearing small frowns, and Olive Reamer's eyes focused on Yuma. The old man's weathered face wore an expression of distaste, as though he were smelling a dead fish.

"Do you agree with the captain's analysis of the Apache, Mister Kelly?" Olive Reamer asked.

"Not especially," Yuma remarked.

"Do you agree that there are differences among them?" she pressed.

"The Jicarilla kill out of habit, the White Mountain Apache kill for fun, the Chiricahua do it out of hate, and the Mescalero make killing a religion," Yuma said.

"Then you're saying there's really no difference, for all practical purposes," Olive concluded.

"Not unless you care whether you're slit from throat to crotch the way the Chiricahua do it, or from crotch to throat the way the Mescalero like doing it," Yuma said.

Capt. Ellwood's face had grown stiff, his anger barely contained. "Do you have anything else to report or contribute, Fargo?" the captain bit out.

Fargo hesitated for a moment and decided against bringing up Blossom. "Not now," he said.

"Will you help us track down my brother, Captain?" the senator asked. "I'd be real appreciative of anything you can do."

"I'll put a full troop at your disposal, lead them out with you myself," the captain said. "We'll find your brother."

Fargo saw Robertson and Downs exchange quick

glances. "We're most appreciative of that, too, Captain," Downs said.

"I'll need the day to take care of things here, but we can leave in the morning," Capt. Ellwood said, his smooth face relaxed again.

Fargo saw Jim Robertson stand, his tweed jacket fall open, and he glimpsed a shoulder holster with a hammerless, short-barreled five-shot Colt ejector revolver. Robertson's jacket closed again as he turned.

Olive Reamer come up to Fargo, her full red lips holding the hint of a wry smile. "You don't think much of Captain Ellwood, do you?" she commented, and he decided that Olive Reamer was the sharpest of all the others.

"He's a square peg in a round hole," Fargo said. "A lost sheep out here."

"Experience is the best teacher," the woman said.

"If he can stay alive that long," Fargo said.

Olive Reamer turned her gaze to Yuma. "What do you think the chances are for finding Dale Talbot alive?" she asked.

"About the same as finding a live chicken in a hawk's nest," Yuma answered.

Olive frowned into space. "As the senator said, we must go on. We must find out one way or the other," she said, and her eyes met Fargo's gaze. "I'm glad you're coming along," she said, and in the brown eyes he caught the faint flicker of deep fire.

"Olive," the senator called out, and she turned away.

Fargo walked beside Yuma to their horses.

"Why didn't you say anything about the girl?" Yuma asked.

"Blossom?" Fargo smiled. "Decided it might be more interesting to spring her on them in person."

"You smell a rat someplace in this thing?" Yuma questioned.

"Don't know," Fargo said. "But something isn't right. Can't put my finger on it yet, but I feel it."

"Man and his niece want to find a brother. Nothin' wrong with that," Yuma said with an edge of amusement in his voice. "Two men from a bank trying to get their important papers back. Nothin' wrong in that."

"Not on the face of it, and don't bait me, you old fox," Fargo said, and heard Yuma's chuckle. "You know they all seem awful anxious to find a man likely past finding alive, and I saw you take in those two bank men. They don't set right."

"They don't, but then I'm no expert on bankers. What are you thinking?" Yuma asked.

"I'm thinking they sure as hell look more like Pinkerton men than bankers to me," Fargo answered.

"Dammed if they don't," Yuma agreed.

"The senator didn't seem at all happy to see them. I got the feeling he had the same suspicion," Fargo said. "Which means nobody's exactly telling the truth about this search for Dale Talbot."

"You figure to play along for now?" Yuma asked.

"For now," Fargo said.

"What about the boy captain? Think he smells a rat, too?"

"Hell, no. He's too busy trying to impress the others to see his nose in front of his face," Fargo answered.

"I'll nose around some this afternoon. See you come morning," Yuma said as he swung his long, spare frame onto the quarter horse and rode from the barracks.

Fargo took the Ovaro by the cheek strap and led the horse to the boardinghouse, where he dropped the reins over the hitching post and went inside. He knocked at the door of Room Four and it was opened almost instantly. Blossom, her thick blond hair a golden shawl around her face, wore a white shirt and dark skirt, and looked lovely as a marsh marigold.

"Been waiting for you," she said with such sweetness he felt suspicious at once. She closed the door, turned to him, and only his instant, catlike reflexes let him avoid the blow she aimed at his cheek. "Bastard!" Blossom spit at him, her face sudden fury. "What were you doing at the stable last night? Don't deny it. The stableman told me this morning."

"Your horse looked as if he needed a good rubdown and curry. I was doing you a favor," Fargo said calmly.

"Hell you were. You were sneaking around trying to find out something. You told the stableman I asked you to curry him," Blossom spit back.

"I figured he might give me a hard time otherwise," Fargo said.

"Liar. You just wanted to sneak around my things," Blossom said.

"You've a suspicious mind, Blossom," Fargo chided. "I was just trying to do you a favor. Did you look at the horse? See anything wrong with him?"

"Yes, I did, and he's fine, but you're still lying. Maybe you wanted to go through my personal things. If you did, you found out I had them all with me," she snapped.

Fargo shrugged. "Never thought about it," he said. It was plain she had decided he hadn't looked in the extra pack. She put her hands on her hips and the points of her breasts touched the white shirt.

"You know, I decided I really wanted you to come back today," she said. "I was looking forward to it, believe it or not. But you blew that with your sneaking around at my things."

"Too bad." Fargo shrugged. "See you around." He turned away and started for the door.

"What about your meeting?" Blossom asked sharply.

"None of your concern, honey," he said, and swallowed the doorknob in one big hand.

"Wait," Blossom called out. He halted, his hand still around the doorknob as he looked sideways at her. Her glare was a half-pout. "Maybe it is of my concern," she muttered.

Fargo let go of the doorknob and turned to her, a thin smile touching his lips. "An attack of honesty? That's an improvement," he commented. "Where do you fit in with Dale Talbot?"

"Tell me about the meeting," she said.

"Ladies first," he growled.

Her face remained tight and yet stayed lovely, something few women could pull off, he decided. "All right, I came out to find Dale Talbot," Blossom said. "I'll tell you that much."

"Tell me something I didn't figure out already," Fargo said. "Why?"

"That's personal, and it doesn't matter," she said.

"Everything matters," he returned.

"Look, I just want to find him—alive, I hope," Blossom said, and he caught the note of despair in her voice.

"The line forms at the right," Fargo said.

"What do you mean?" She frowned.

"The meeting was crowded," Fargo told her. "Senator Talbot was there; his niece, Olive Reamer, was there; and so were two bank men from Virginia—everybody wanting to find Dale Talbot."

"His niece? Is that what he called her?" Blossom frowned.

"You know Olive Reamer?"

"She's been the senator's secretary and right-hand girl for years," Blossom said.

"What about the two bank men?" Fargo questioned.

"I don't know what they're doing out here," Blossom said, and the bewilderment in her voice was real.

"But you seem to know a fair amount about the senator," Fargo reminded her.

"I used to visit Washington a lot," Blossom said quickly.

"The senator had the brains to come out and try to get some help. How'd you expect to trail Apache and find Dale Talbot all by your lost little self?" Fargo frowned.

"I thought I could do it. I thought it out carefully and planned every step," she said.

"So I noticed," Fargo said wryly.

The very blue eyes flared. "Things can go wrong. That's why I came back to Adobles with you. I realized it wouldn't be as easy as I thought. I want you to find the Apache who took Dale and I'll do the rest. I'll pay you, Fargo. Two hundred dollars. That's a lot of money."

"The army's hired me to help them find Talbot," Fargo said.

"A doctor has more than one patient. A trailsman can have more than one client," Blossom shot back.

"I want more answers. Why do you want to find Dale Talbot?" he asked.

"I told you, why isn't important. Just find him," she said.

"I don't go chasing a pig in a poke, honey." He saw her lips tighten.

"Maybe later, when I know you better, I'll say more. Two hundred dollars ought to let me keep what I want to myself. Meanwhile, you just find the Apache for me," Blossom said.

"Why do I think there's something more than love and concern for Dale Talbot in this here search?" he asked mildly.

"I've my reasons. Other people have theirs. I don't know what they are," Blossom said.

The answer was too glib and Fargo kept the smile to himself, let tiny thoughts turn in his head. She wasn't giving him all of it, but she admitted as much. However, she wasn't the only one playing games. The others wore masks too, and they were staying completely hidden behind them. Fargo grimaced angrily. He wasn't going Apache hunting without knowing the real reason for it, and Blossom could be the way to tear off those masks. He brought his attention back to Blossom and saw her eyes round and waiting.

"I guess I could take you along," he said.

Her arms were around his neck instantly, her lips pressing hard against his. He felt her lips open and the tip of her tongue slide out. "You figuring this'll get you special treatment, you're all wrong," he said.

"I'm not thinking that," she said.

"I don't believe you." He grinned.

"I don't believe your story about rubbing my horse down," she half-pouted.

"That makes us even," he said, and curled his hand around her neck and drew her to him. His mouth pressed down on hers and she responded at once. His other hand moved along the collar of the shirt, down the neckline, and flicked at the buttons. The shirt fell open and her breasts came forward, a little long but gracefully curved with long, smooth lines and tiny pink tips on lighter pink circles. His hand cupped one, his thumb gliding over the tiny tip, which instantly began to grow firm.

"You going to stay all dressed up like that," Blossom murmured.

"Didn't expect to," Fargo said as he stepped back and shed his clothes. He watched Blossom curl up on the bed, undo her skirt, and pull off her pink bloomers. She put her head back and shook the thick, long blond hair. Fargo, naked, moved to her as he took in the loveliness of her: slightly curved belly, a modest dark nap just below it, and firm thighs that curved beautifully into long calves. He saw her glance at him as he sank down beside her, and the eager appreciation leapt into her eyes. Her hand reached out at once, curled around the firm-fleshed organ that beckoned to her.

"Oh, jeez," Blossom breathed as she clasped him to her, pressing his maleness against the soft curve of her pubic mound. His mouth found one long breast, drew it in, and he felt her back arch in pleasure. "Ah, ah . . . jeez," she breathed again as he pulled her breast deep into his mouth, let his lips nibble on the tiny tip, his tongue circle its pink firmness. He felt Blossom's hands moving to his buttocks, pulling him over onto her as she fell onto her back. "Quick, Fargo, please . . . oh, please," she cried out and her firm thighs opened for him, closed, fell open again.

He felt the tightness of her hands now against his back and her body lifting upward to push against him. She moved her hips, a half-rotation movement, as she sought to find him and he moved with her, let his pulsating organ rest against the dark portal. "Aaaah . . . ah, yes, now, please now, oh, God," Blossom gasped, and the blond hair tossed wildly against the sheet. She thrust up onto him and he let himself enter, feeling the warmth of her. A cry of desire rose from her lips as he thrust forward, and he felt her thighs clasp around him as though to make certain he wouldn't slip from her.

She pushed up as he went forward, a sharp, sudden movement, repeated instantly. "Harder, Fargo," Blossom half-gasped. "Harder." He drew back and rammed forward, again, and then again. "Yes, yes, oh, ah . . . aaaah," Blossom cried out with each ramming thrust. Her lips sought his face as he bent down, caressing the long breasts with his tongue, and he felt the thick blond hair cascade around his head. Blossom's frenzied wanting suddenly turned wild, and he felt her thighs tighten around him. "Keep on, keep on," she muttered between gasps. "More, more . . . oh, oh, more." He was ramming hard into her as he felt her grow rigid, her hands dig into his back. She slammed her pelvis upward against him as he felt the contractions tightening around his still-thrusting organ. "Yes, yes . . . now, now . . . oh, good God, aaaaaaaah . . ." Blossom screamed, and she clasped herself to him as the spiraling ecstasy consumed, flamed, and then, too quickly, vanished. "Damn," Blossom protested as she sank back onto the bed, suddenly depleted, breathing hard.

He smiled down at her warm beauty as he lay propped up on one elbow beside her. "Didn't expect you were going to be in such a hurry," he commented.

"Neither did I," Blossom said. "I saw you and it all just sort of swept over me."

He smiled down at her as she stretched, the movement provocative and catlike, and he saw that darkness had lowered itself outside the window.

"A little afternoon delight helps pass the day," he said.

"It sure does," Blossom echoed. "You've someplace else to go?"

"Not especially," he said, and Blossom's little smile was smug. She moved, brought herself over him, lowered her face to his, and once again he felt the long blond hair tumble over him. She moved one leg slowly up and down his thighs. "Stay the night, Fargo," she murmured.

"Why not?" He shrugged. "Could be a long time between drinks."

"Not tonight," she said as she lifted one breast to his lips.

4

The morning light filtered through the lone window of the room. He was up, washed, and dressed before Blossom stirred and opened her eyes. She focused on his tall figure, and her eyes cast aside sleep at once as she leapt from the bed, long breasts swaying beautifully. "Why didn't you wake me?" she complained.

"Relax. You've plenty of time," he told her. "I want you to hang back until you see the troop riding out with the others. Then you come along."

She cast him a sidelong glance as she walked to the big, white ceramic basin of water atop the dresser. "Why?" she questioned.

"Because that's the way I want it, honey," he said. "And I don't expect to have to explain everything I do or say."

"You've a reason, I know that much," she said sulkily as she scooped water from the basin with her hands and pressed her face into both palms.

"Go to the head of the class," Fargo answered.

She brought her head up, her face wet and shining, to frown at him. "No tricks," she muttered.

"God, you're as suspicious as you are hard-nosed. No tricks," he said. She was also too nakedly delicious to stay with, and he flung the door open and hurried outside.

He had time to give the Ovaro a quick brushing and then walked the horse toward the army post at the end of town. He saw Yuma talking to two men at the head of a line of three wagons drawn up outside the barracks building. He then let his eyes scan the wagons. All three were Owensboro Texas cotton-bed wagons with their high sides and extra deep bodies, and all had been outfitted with canvas stretched over bows. A few men and too many women and children peered out at him as he led the Ovaro past to halt beside Yuma.

"Jeb White and Zach Diamond," Yuma said, gesturing to the two men. "This is Fargo, the man I told you about," he added.

"Howdy," said Jeb White, a thin man with a thin face and black hair. "You're the one they call the Trailsman."

"These good folks have themselves a problem. They're out to reach a new settlement on the other side of the Sacramento Mountains. But to get there they have to go right through Mescalero country," Yuma said. "The Apache have wiped out every group that's tried to get through this year. They came here because they understood the army would give them protection through the route."

Fargo's eyes went to Jeb White and Zach Diamond, a short man with tired eyes in a worn, tired face. "What made you understand that?" he asked. "Seeing as how they didn't escort any of the other wagon trains."

"The others never stopped to ask," Jeb White answered. "We stopped at Fort Dodd up Oklahoma way and spoke to the commander there."

"He tell you to expect an escort?" Fargo frowned.

"He told us that it was up to the field commander but that it was army policy to protect all settlers in the territories. Said it was in army rules and policies, he did," Jeb answered.

"I know what it says there," Fargo commented. "And the captain turned you down."

"That's right. He told us he didn't have the extra men to spare," Jeb White answered, and Fargo caught Yuma's glance as he let his lips purse. "We went and did other things," the man added.

"But I'm worried. Ned and Vera should've been back a half-hour ago," Zach Diamond said, and Fargo saw him peer down the long main street of the town.

"Back from where?" Fargo asked.

"We decided to try to hire us our own protection, at least a half-dozen men to ride guard for us through Mescalero country. Ned Snyder went hiring and took a girl from the wagons with him to take down names. Ned doesn't hardly write," Zach said.

"You can't pay enough to hire most men to go into Mescalero country," Fargo said. "Where'd your people go looking?"

"The saloon. We figured that'd be the best place to find hands for hire," Zach said.

"Not this early in the day," Fargo said, and saw the worry lines digging into the man's brow.

"They should've been back. We'd best go see what's wrong," he muttered. "Guess it'll be all right to leave the others in the wagons here by the post."

"Stay with them. I'll go look for you. What's Ned Snyder like?" Fargo said.

"Medium height, bald as a billiard ball. The girl's name is Vera, right pretty, dark hair, wearing a tan shirt," Zach answered, and Fargo climbed onto his horse and sent the steed cantering down Main Street.

Adobles' saloon and dance hall was at the other end of the town and, in a bow to the past and the present, was called the Yanqui Saloon. Otherwise, it was indistinguishable from a thousand other dance-hall saloons. Fargo drew to a halt before it, slipped from the saddle, and strode into the building. There were only a few figures in the big room, the bartender behind the bar, a watery-eyed figure huddled over a beer at one of the tables, and two porters sweeping the floor with wide, long-handled brooms. Fargo's glance swept the room again and halted at the bartender. The man's stare was cautious and appraising as he rested a rag on top of the bar. "Looking for a bald man and a dark-haired girl," Fargo said.

The bartender shrugged and looked away, but not before Fargo caught the quick flicker in his eyes. Fargo's eyes scanned the two porters. They were pushing their brooms faster, with increased concentration. Fargo felt a tiny warning tremor, that sixth sense he had learned never to discount. Something was wrong, he muttered silently, and brought his eyes back to the bartender. "Bald man and girl with a tan shirt," he repeated.

The bartender didn't look at him as he began to polish the top of the bar with the rag. "You don't see them, they're not here," he said.

"They came here," Fargo answered, and felt uneasiness stabbing at him.

The bartender continued to concentrate on polishing the bar. "Don't remember," he said, not looking up.

The uneasiness turned into alarm inside Fargo, intuition snapping itself into instant sensitivity. "You don't have that many customers not to remember," he said, an edge coming into his voice. The bartender made no reply as he continued to polish the bar, and Fargo turned to the two porters. They had halted to stare at him, but they turned away at once and began pushing their brooms. "You, in the overalls, you see a bald man and a girl?" Fargo called.

The porter paused and looked up, and Fargo saw that the fear in the man's dull eyes was real. "Didn't see anybody . . . not me," the man mumbled.

They were lying, all of them, Fargo realized, and moving with sudden speed, he took two long strides to the bar. The bartender heard him coming, dropped his bar rag, and started to reach under the bar. Fargo's arms shot out and he closed both hands around the man's neck and yanked. The bartender came halfway over the bar and Fargo saw the cut-down shotgun fall from the man's hands as it hit against the edge of the bar. "What happened to them?" Fargo rasped.

The man, his torso over the bar, managed his answer through a squeezed throat. "Don't know. You're crazy, mister," he said.

Fargo stepped back and pulled the bartender with him. He let go as the man came over the front of the bar and the figure dropped, landed on the floor on hands and knees. Fargo brought his right knee up, a hard, short motion that crashed under the bartender's jaw. The man's head snapped up and back as he collapsed to the floor. Fargo whirled, one hand on the butt of the big Colt .45 at his side, to see the two porters staring at him. He speared the one with the overalls with an icy stare. "What happened to the man and the girl?" he growled. "You've got three seconds to answer."

The man's fear-filled eyes blinked. "The Torrance brothers," he mumbled, his voice quivering.

"What's that mean?" Fargo barked.

"The Torrance brothers took them both. They wanted the girl," the man said. "The Torrance brothers are mean varmints. The man and the girl just came in here and they pounced right on them."

"Where'd they take them?" Fargo pressed.

"That way," the porter said, gesturing with his head to a rear door. "Probably inside the old woodshed out back."

Fargo spun, raced out the rear door of the saloon to see the old woodshed directly in his path. A door hung half off the dilapidated structure, and he was at it in three long strides. He slowed, slipped through the opened doorway, and heard the muffled scream from the depths of the old shed. The inside of the abandoned structure was dim, light slipping through cracks between the warped boards, and he heard the girl's muffled cry again. It came from behind a cross-lattice of old beams and loose lengths of lumber that still cluttered the floor, and he moved to a narrow space at the side of the shed where he could peer into the rear section.

He saw Ned Snyder first, unconscious, a red laceration across the top of his bald pate that bore the marks of a gun-butt blow. He peered past the man's still form on the floor to where three men struggled with the girl almost against the rear wall. They had her down on the floor and he saw the kerchief tied over her mouth. Two were holding her, one at the shoulders, the other hanging on to her legs as she tried to struggle. The third Torrance brother had just shed trousers and B.V.D. bottoms and stood naked from the waist down. "Take her legs," he ordered, and the one let go of her shoulders and seized her left leg while the second clasped her right leg. "Pull 'em open," the third brother ordered, and dropped down half over the girl as she started to sit up and claw at her attackers. He seized her arms and pinned her back to the floor. "Don't fight it baby. Just enjoy it. I got something special for you," he said. His words ended in a sharp grunt as the girl got one knee up and slammed it into his ribs. "Hold her, goddammit," he swore at his brothers. He wriggled himself backward as the other two yanked her legs down and apart.

Fargo drew the big Colt .45, held it for a moment, and let it drop back into its holster with a silent curse. The angle was bad and they were all over the girl. A heavy slug from the .45 could go right through one and into her.

"Look at this, baby," the third Torrance brother chortled as he came down on his knees over the girl. "Look what's waiting for you."

Fargo glanced to his side, seized a two-by-four, and on silent cat's feet, crossed the few yards of the back of the old shed. The third Torrance's bare buttocks, heavy, fleshy, rough-skinned orbs, rose up in the air. He paused, positioned himself as he flipped the girl's skirt up and tore her white undergarments away. Fargo glimpsed her round little belly for an instant. "Here it comes, baby," the man half-laughed.

"That's right, you bastard," Fargo growled as he swung the two-by-four with both hands. It slammed into the back of the man's bare legs just below his buttocks.

"Ow, Christ," Torrance screamed as he fell backward. He rolled from the girl as he clutched at the back of his legs with both hands. His two brothers released their hold on the girl as they spun around, surprise on their slack-jawed faces.

Fargo rammed the two-by-four forward and drove it into the nearest one's face. The bridge of the man's nose cracked with a sharp sound and he spurted blood from both nostrils and both cheekbones. His half-scream of pain was a guttural gasp as he fell on his side and clutched at his face. Fargo's eyes flicked to the half-naked brother, saw the man still on the floor rubbing the back of his legs. He turned his gaze to the one he hadn't touched yet, and saw the man had his gun out from its holster. Fargo swung the length of wood in a sideways arc and it cracked against the man's hand as he brought the gun up to fire. The man cursed in pain as the gun fell from his fingers. He tried to dive for it, but Fargo brought the two-by-four down across

71

the back of his neck. The brother hit the floor on his face and lay still.

Fargo turned at a movement behind him, and saw the third Torrance brother diving at him, his naked lower extremities churning as he dug his feet hard into the dirt flooring. "Bastard. Goddamn son of a bitch," the man yelled as he dived. Fargo dropped to one knee, shifted the length of lumber so that Torrance dived into it at crotch level. "Aaaah, Jesus, owooo," Torrance yelled as he collapsed and rolled on the floor, both hands grasping his crotch. "Oh, Jesus, oh, Christ," he wailed in pain as he drew his legs up. He writhed in pain on the floor and Fargo tossed the two-by-four aside. It'd be a long time before the man could do anything more than think about a woman, he spat inwardly as his eyes lifted to see the girl on her feet, pulling her clothes in place.

Zach Diamond hadn't exaggerated her prettiness. Dark hair and brown eyes were set in a round face with a small, delicate nose and full red lips. Her figure echoed her face, all rounded and full with firm, round breasts and good, well-fleshed hips, a sensuousness just behind the young openness of her. "You all right?" he asked.

"Because of you." She nodded as she stepped around the writhing Torrance brother. "What made you come here?" she asked, standing very close to him, her round brown eyes searching his face, taking in the strong, handsome chiseled lines.

"Came looking for you," Fargo said, and a tiny furrow came to her brow. "Zach Diamond and Jeb White told me where you and Ned Snyder had gone. They were worried when you didn't come back."

A groan from one of the other Torrance brothers interrupted, and Fargo stepped to Ned Snyder's still-unconscious form. "Let's get out of here. I'll take him, you follow," he said, and lifted the man over his shoulder. He returned to where he'd entered the old wood-shed, went outside, and skirted the saloon to circle to the hitching post in front. "Where are your horses?" he asked the girl.

"We came on foot," she said as he lay the unconscious form over the Ovaro's saddle. "Will he be all right?" she asked.

Fargo lifted the man's eyelid and peered at him. "He'll have himself a headache for a day or so," he told her.

"I'm Vera Harper," she said, standing in front of him, her eyes very round as she gazed up at him.

"Fargo. Sky Fargo," he returned.

"You a friend of Jeb and Zach?" Vera asked.

"Just happened to be talking to them," he said.

Vera's hand came to rest on his arm. "Lucky for me. I can't do much but say thanks to you," she said.

"Don't need more," he told her.

Her hand stayed on his arm, a faint but firm pressure. She reached up and brushed his cheek with her lips, a touch as soft as a butterfly's wing. "You deserve more," she said, and her round brown eyes were filled with a kind of honest innocence as she stepped back. She was a combination of innocence and simmering sensuousness, he decided, the woman in her pushing through the almost little-girl-like outward surface. She fell in beside him as he took the pinto by the cheek strap and began to lead the horse back toward the army post, her full, rounded figure brushing lightly against him as she walked.

"You heard why Ned and I came to the saloon?" Vera asked. He nodded and saw the flash of bitterness flood into her face. "One more thing that didn't work out," she said.

"Such as?" he asked.

"The army refusing to give us an escort," she said. "My fiancé up and dying along the way." Fargo's frown questioned. "He and I started out together, but he came down with the fever in Kansas and died in Oklahoma."

"You decided to go on."

She half-shrugged. "No place else to go. My folks are in that new settlement we're trying to reach."

"And you'll go on even though the army's not going to give you an escort?" Fargo asked.

Her round, grave eyes wore pain in their depths. "The others are the same as I am. Nobody's got anyplace or anything left to go back to. We've got to go on," she said. "Our hope is in that settlement on the other side of the Sacramento range."

He was saved from having to comment as they reached the wagons and he saw others rush out to lift Ned Snyder from the saddle. Jeb White halted beside Fargo, and Vera told him what had happened. When she finished, Jeb's eyes probed the big man's chiseled face. "We're beholden to you, Fargo," he said. "Zach and I were thinking while you were out finding Ned and Vera. We'll pay you all we can put together if you could get the captain to give us that escort. Your friend Yuma tells me the captain's kind of depending on you for help."

Fargo's smile was rueful. "Yuma knows it, I know it, but the captain thinks he doesn't need anybody but himself," Fargo said. "But I'll give it a try."

"We'd appreciate that," Jeb White said, and Fargo beckoned to Yuma as he started toward the barracks. "Let's pay the captain a visit," he said.

"Got something to tell you first," Yuma said, dropping his voice to a half-whisper as they walked. "I got hold of that old booze-hound Johnny Kelter, loosened him up with a half-dozen shots of rotgut. The Apache that took Dale Talbot were Mescalero."

"That's more than just whiskey talk?" Fargo questioned.

Yuma drew a torn piece of calfskin moccasin from his pocket, and Fargo immediately saw the half-moon design cut into the material. "Kelter came out from hiding when they left. He found this. Mescalero markings," Yuma grunted.

Fargo nodded. "Good work," he said. "We'll just keep this to ourselves for now."

Yuma grunted in agreement and followed him onto the post grounds.

The senator was outside the captain's quarters helping Olive Reamer with a stubborn cinch ring. She wore a brown riding outfit, tailored like the one she'd worn the day before, her hair held back by a brown ribbon. She smiled at Fargo and he was aware again of the sensuousness behind the severity of her tailored clothes. Not the open, innocent sensuousness that was Vera Harper. Olive Reamer gave out a contained, controlled sensuousness that held experience and amused interest.

"We've been waiting for you," the senator said with annoyance.

"Waiting's good practice. Makes a man patient," Fargo answered as he walked past and heard Olive Reamer's soft chuckle. In the office, the captain looked up from his desk as Fargo entered with Yuma.

"Got a wagon train on your doorstep, I see," Fargo said. "They told me they'd been in to see you."

"Then they told you what I said to them," Capt. Ellwood answered coldly.

"They did." Fargo smiled. "Surprised me some."

The captain frowned at him. "Why?" he questioned.

"Seeing as how I figured you for a man who'd follow army policies," Fargo said. "If I remember, the regulations say the army shall aid, assist, protect, and otherwise encourage all civilians in developing new settlements whenever possible."

He saw Capt. Ellwood's face draw righteous authority around itself at once. "I don't need you to quote army policies to me, Fargo," he snapped. "Policy also is clear that the decisions are the responsibility of the commander in the field, and that is me. I haven't any more men to spare on special details. I have to keep regular patrols out."

"Those folks are going to be massacred," Yuma said.

"They can turn back. I've already committed myself to helping the senator," the captain returned icily. "That decision is mine to make."

"Guess so," Fargo said.

"I remind you, despite general army policy, I am not obligated to provide an escort for every band of ragtag settlers that come this way." The captain frowned.

"Or every senator," Fargo returned, and saw the captain's smooth face redden.

"We'll be heading out at once, Fargo," Capt. Ellwood snapped in dismissal, and Fargo turned, strode out of the office, Yuma hurrying to stay alongside him.

"What's he got against settlers?" Yuma growled.

"Nothing, but a friendly senator in Washington can help a lot when promotion time comes around. Settlers can't do a damn thing for him but be grateful," Fargo answered.

"The little bastard," Yuma swore softly.

"Maybe we can make a real officer out of him yet," Fargo said as he halted at the Ovaro.

The troop was lined up two abreast, a square-jawed sergeant holding the captain's horse. The senator, Olive Reamer, and the two bank men waited a dozen feet from the column of soldiers. Fargo's eyes went to the distant wagons as the captain came from his office.

"We just forget about those poor folks?" Yuma asked.

"No," Fargo murmured as he saw Vera, her wide eyes and firm, round figure easy to pick out. "You get over there and give them a message. Tell them to do exactly as I say and I'll help them get through Mescalero country when the time comes."

"I'm listenin'," Yuma said, and Fargo leaned closer, his words quick, terse, and Yuma nodded in understanding when he finished. "Got it. I'll catch up to you in a minute," Yuma said, and started for the wagons in a half-lope, half-run.

Fargo swung onto the Ovaro when Capt. Ellwood wheeled his horse to the head of the column. The captain raised his arm and the sergeant barked orders. The column moved forward and Fargo watched the troop march past. Most of the men wore enough years of field experience in their faces, he was glad to see, and he waited to let the senator and the others pull in before he swung the Ovaro alongside. "Northwest," he said to Capt. Ellwood.

"Why?" the captain asked with faint disdain.

"Got my reasons," Fargo said.

"I should like to hear them," the captain said.

"When the time comes," Fargo answered.

The captain was about to insist on another answer when Olive Reamer's voice cut in. "Do you have a reason to go in any other direction, Captain?" she asked with sweet firmness.

"No, ma'am," the captain said, and turned away, his jaw set tight.

Yuma saw Blossom riding toward them from the right rear before any of the others noticed, Fargo realized, and the old man leaned toward him in the saddle.

"You expecting company?" he whispered, and Fargo let his smile answer. "Springing her as a surprise, eh? Why?" Yuma asked.

"Want to see everybody's reaction firsthand," Fargo replied.

Blossom rode up, her blond hair tossing, and flung a brilliant smile at the captain as he brought the column to a halt. Fargo looked to the senator and the others. The two bank men regarded her with a mixture of interest and curiosity, but the senator's face grew rigid as it turned red, and Fargo saw the man hold back words with an effort. He glanced at Olive Reamer and saw her staring at Blossom with narrowed eyes, her full lips drawn in on each other. Fargo smiled inwardly. He had his answer. Both the senator and Olive knew Blossom—or at least who she was—their reactions too quick to disguise. And that meant that Blossom knew the senator from more than just his picture in the Washington papers.

"Can I help you, miss?" Fargo heard the captain ask Blossom.

"I'm with him," she said, pointing to the big man with the lake-blue eyes. "I hired him to find Dale Talbot for me," she said with another broad smile.

The captain's brows lifted as he looked at Fargo. "Is this true?" he asked, and Fargo nodded. "But you're under contract to the army." Capt. Ellwood frowned.

"Nothing says I can't have more than one client," Fargo answered, making use of Blossom's logic. "Especially since she wants the same thing everyone else here does."

The captain's frown remained as he glanced back to Blossom. "I don't know that this is in order at all," he said, and Fargo saw Blossom toss another smile at him. "What's your interest in finding Dale Talbot, Miss . . . ?" he asked.

"Daley, Blossom Daley," she said. "Dale was my very best friend. When I heard what had happened to him, I just had to come out to see if I could find him and help him."

Fargo almost snickered. It was more of a reason than she'd given him, but as phony as a three-dollar bill. The senator knew that much also, and Olive's faint grimace of disdain gave away her thoughts. Even Downs and Robertson exchanged cautious glances.

Only the captain, in his pompous naïveté, appeared to swallow Blossom's answer whole. "It's mighty foolish of you to come out here all by yourself, Miss Daley," he said.

"That's why I hired Fargo," Blossom said, and gave the captain another dazzling smile. "Now, with your troop along, I know I'll be safe," she said.

Capt. Ellwood straightened in the saddle. "I'll do my best to see to that," he said, then turned to Fargo. "This is highly irregular, but out of concern for this young lady, I'll go along with it. Let's move," he said, and glanced back at the column.

Fargo saw the surprised frown come over his face as he saw the three wagons rolling along behind them, still a good distance back.

"What are they doing?" he muttered. "Sergeant, keep the column moving," he ordered, turned his mount, and headed back toward the distant wagons. Fargo and Yuma swung in behind the captain, cantered up to him as he rode and drew a sharp glance.

Jeb White in the lead wagon drew to a halt as the captain approached, and Fargo saw Vera peer out at him from the third wagon, her brown eyes round as saucers.

"I told you I wasn't providing an escort for you people," the captain barked at Jeb.

"We heard you," Jeb answered.

"What are you doing here?" the captain asked.

"Going the same way, it seems," Jeb answered mildly.

"You're following my troop," the captain snapped.

"It's a free country, Captain. We can go anywhere we like," Jeb said.

"The man's right, sonny," Yuma cut in, and received a glare from the captain.

"Did you put them up to this, Fargo?" the captain accused.

Fargo let himself look aggrieved. "You've got a suspicious turn of mind, Captain," he said.

The officer snorted in disgust, spun his mount, and galloped away.

Jeb's glance at Fargo held a smile as he rolled the wagons forward. Vera came past in the last wagon and leaned out, the motion pulling the tan shirt tight against her full, round breasts.

"Can you come visit tonight?" she called.

"I'll try," Fargo said, and rode off with Yuma beside him. When they reached the column, he swung alongside Olive Reamer. Senator Talbot's face remained tight with anger, he saw, but Olive's smile was relaxed and inviting.

"How did Miss Daley find you, Fargo?" she asked.

"Just came up to me in town," he lied. "Said she'd heard about me."

"She give you the same story she gave Captain Ellwood?" Olive asked.

"Yes." Fargo nodded. "Why? Something wrong with it?"

Olive fielded the question with ease, he noted. "I wouldn't know about that," she said. "But somehow I think there is. Woman's intuition. Maybe you should be careful of her."

"I'll remember that," Fargo said. "Should I be careful of you too?" he slid at her.

"Perhaps, but not for the same reasons." Olive smiled and gave him a sidelong glance. "I find you fascinating. You're playing the captain the way a fisherman plays a trout. Are you as fascinating in other ways?"

"Absolutely," Fargo answered.

"You don't believe in modesty, I see," Olive Reamer said, and smiled.

"Truth's better." He laughed and sent the pinto into a canter. He moved past Blossom as she rode beside the captain; he nodded to her and went on as Yuma caught up to him. "Spread out," he said, and Yuma turned his horse to canter off to the right. Fargo took the left point and rode on, his eyes sweeping the low dunes and the pointed hillocks. He scanned the dry soil as he traveled, increased his pace, and rose up on the top of a dune to see Yuma's distant figure halted near a line of giant saguaro cactus. He steered the Ovaro toward Yuma and came to a halt where Yuma gestured to a trail of unshod prints across the ground.

"Maybe six hours old," Yuma said.

"Think they're watching us from someplace?" Fargo asked as his eyes moved over the tall sandstone pinnacles.

"Can't say. But they will be tomorrow," Yuma answered.

Fargo nodded agreement, aware that they'd be into Mescalero country by morning. He found a small trickle of water and waited for the others to catch up and let the horses drink.

Blossom sidled over to him with a sly little smile "I'd say I did right well," she told him. "And Captain Ellwood's cute. A little stiff, but I can unbend him."

"Good," Fargo said. "He was the only one who swallowed that story. The senator was definitely unhappy to see you. Why?"

Blossom shrugged, tossed her thick blond hair. "I don't know. He probably would be unhappy to see anybody," she said.

81

Fargo nodded and smiled as he signaled to Yuma and rode on.

"She's still playing her own games," he said to Yuma. "And she's working hard to add the captain as insurance."

"You calling her hand soon, Fargo?" Yuma questioned, and the big man nodded. "I'm sure of one thing. Not one of them has given the real reason they're chasin' after a man more likely dead than alive," Yuma added.

Fargo grunted agreement and pointed to a row of low dunes that rose ahead. "You take the left ones, I'll take the right," he said, and sent the Ovaro into a canter.

There was a line of unshod hoofprints across the top of one dune, but nothing else caught his eye. The day wore to an end as he crossed back on the other side of the dunes to where Yuma had halted at a long line of sandstone pillars that formed a good spot to camp. Fargo dismounted, unsaddled the pinto, and sat against one of the rock formations in the dying light as the column arrived.

"Army rations for everybody," the captain said as he lined the mounts up along the sandstone.

Fargo watched as Blossom carefully took the extra pack from the big gray's rump and put it on the ground with her saddlebag. Olive Reamer sat down near the senator while Downs and Robertson stayed together. The troopers made their own small fire, and Capt. Ellwood joined the senator as he handed out rations.

"Eat with us, Captain," Blossom said, and the captain was quick to accept, settling down beside her. Fargo had just finished his beef jerky when the senator, irritation still in his round face and voice, lifted his stentorian voice.

"Robertson, what kind of work did my brother do for the bank?" he asked.

"Confidential work for the president," Robertson said without hesitation.

"Funny he never mentioned it to me," Sen. Talbot returned.

"He was sworn not to talk about it to anyone," Downs interjected calmly.

The senator made an impatient sound and turned his irritableness on the captain. "I'd like to know how you expect to find out which Apache band took Dale, Captain," he snapped.

"I'll make contact, capture at least one, and interrogate him," the captain said.

Yuma made a derisive sound. "Interrogate him? Why not do somethin' easy and get answers out of a tortoise?" he commented.

"How would you go about it, Mister Kelly?" Olive cut in.

"Watch, see if you can spot anything, then move in," Yuma said. "If you take an Apache, you don't interrogate him. You let him know he's a dead man if he doesn't talk."

"Does that work?" Olive asked.

"Only sometimes," Yuma answered.

"I'm sure there are other ways to get an Apache to talk," the senator said.

"There are," Fargo said. "But none guarantees he'll talk and some are worse than Yuma's approach."

"I'm certain I'll be able to interrogate an Apache prisoner," the captain said smugly. He glanced at Fargo and saw the big man's eyes peering past him. He turned to see that the three wagons had halted some fifty yards away and a small cooking fire had already been lighted. He returned an angry frown at Fargo but kept his remarks in check. "I'll be saying good night now," he told the others as he rose to his feet. "I want the men turned in early so they can do a hard day's ride tomorrow."

"No sentries?" Fargo asked mildly.

"I haven't seen a sign of an Apache." Capt. Ellwood frowned.

"Try looking harder," Fargo answered.

"You saw Apache signs?" Blossom questioned, and he nodded.

The senator's voice broke in. "I've always heard Indians don't take much to night fighting," he announced.

"Some don't. The Apache isn't one of them," Fargo said, and pushed himself to his feet. "See you, come morning," he said.

"Where are you going?" Blossom frowned as he started to walk away.

"Visiting," he said.

"Those wagons?" Ambrose Ellwood cut in, and Fargo nodded.

"The dark-haired one?" Blossom said, and his smile admitted surprise. "Saw you talking to her this morning."

The captain's voice interrupted. "It's a very strange coincidence that you've been leading us toward the Sacramento range and that's where those settlers are headed," he said.

"World's full of coincidences." Fargo shrugged.

"You'd better not be taking us out of our way to accommodate those settlers. I wouldn't like that, Fargo," the captain warned.

"I'll try to remember that," Fargo said.

"I wouldn't like that either," Blossom echoed.

"I'll try to remember that too," Fargo answered as he walked on into the darkness. The small cook fire by the wagons had been extinguished, he noted as he strolled closer. The three wagons were still and dark, but he saw Vera emerge from the rear of the one wagon.

"I was watching for you," she said in a half-whisper

84

as she held the canvas flap at the rear of the wagon open for him to enter. He climbed inside and found a place to sink down to the floorboards amid a clutter of boxes, crates, two battered chairs, and a heavy blanket stretched on one side of the wagon that formed a makeshift bed.

Vera sank onto the blanket opposite him, her round, full breasts pushing against a light, gray cotton nightdress tied at the neck with a length of string. "The Simpson kids ride with me in the day, but they go back to their wagon to sleep," she said. "You're wondering why I asked you to come, aren't you?"

"Some," he admitted.

Vera Harper's brown eyes were very round as she studied his face. "I don't know if I can make you understand," she murmured. "I've never explained it, really, not even to myself, never tried to put it into words."

"Try," Fargo said.

"My fiancé was a righteous man. He said it'd be wrong to touch me till after we were married. I didn't have his kind of strength. I just hoped I could wait that long," Vera said, paused, eyeing Fargo with a quick glance. "You think I was wrong for feeling that way?"

"Wouldn't say wrong," he answered. "Some people want more than others."

"Do they ever," Vera burst out almost angrily. "Ever since I was fifteen I've wondered and wanted and waited. I wasn't ever one to throw myself at a man, but that didn't mean I didn't want to know what it was all about. I knew I'd be finding out soon enough after Bill and I got engaged, though I didn't know he was so righteous-minded."

"Then he went and died on you," Fargo supplied.

"Yes, and everything ended then, everything except my wanting. When I heard we might not ever make it to the settlement, I knew I wanted to be made love to before I took an Indian arrow," Vera said, paused to take in a deep breath. "But I knew it couldn't be just anybody. That'd never do. Then, when I saw you, I knew it could be you."

"Why?" he asked.

She shrugged. "Can't say why, really, only that I knew. Something about you, something that just made me know that it could be you, that you'd understand," she said, rushing words together in one long breath. "There, I've said it, and I know it's bold as brass to talk this way, but it seems to me there'd no time left for hiding the way one feels."

"Never had anything against plain talk," Fargo said. "You asking for here and now, Vera?"

She shrugged again, and once more Fargo felt the combination of innocence and throbbing sensuousness that were mixed together in her. "I'll go by what you tell me. You say there's a good chance we'll make it through, and I won't push myself onto you. I'll make myself wait. Can you tell me that, Fargo?" she said.

"Can't promise that," Fargo said. "But you're not pushing yourself on me. You're being plain honest, and it's a compliment you came to me." He reached out, curled his hand around the back of her neck, and drew her to him. "No point in waiting till the last moment, I always say," he murmured as he pressed his mouth to hers.

Vera Harper's full lips stayed motionless for a moment, then suddenly came open, and he felt her arms circle his neck as she returned the kiss with fervor. His finger twisted around the string at the neck of the nightdress and pulled and the garment fell open. He saw the high curve of her breasts, and his hands slipped the loosened garment from her shoulders.

"Oh," Vera gasped, quivered for an instant as the cotton nightdress fell to her waist. Fargo let his eyes take in the beauty of her as he pulled back and began to shed clothes. Vera was made of roundness, everything about her layered with a tiny extra ounce of flesh: soft, rounded shoulders, her breasts full, their cups rounded, skin a soft white with light-pink circles tipped by light-pink nipples. She moved, pushing the nightdress completely from her, and he took in rounded hips, a little rounded belly, and beneath it, a dark, curly tuft that somehow seemed rounded also. She had full legs, soft-fleshed thighs, and fleshy knees. Vera was a perfect example of the flesh following the senses, her body a combination of virginal softness and womanly allure.

Fargo stripped off the last of his clothes, knew he was already responding to the sight of her, and watched as her round eyes grow rounder. "Oh, my. Oh . . . Oh, my," Vera gasped out as she continued to stare at him.

He broke off her stare by pushing her back onto the blanket and curling his hand around one full-cupped breast. He let his fingers caress the soft, smooth white mound, and he traced little circles around the tiny tip. Vera gave out quick, quivering little gasps that became half-cries as he touched the nipple, caressed it with his thumb. When he brought his mouth to it and pulled gently, drawing the soft white breast against his lips, the half-cries became a soft, breathy sound. "Ah . . . ah . . . oh, so nice, oh, so nice . . ." Vera murmured, and he drew the soft mound deeper into his mouth. She gave a half-squeal of newfound delight. He felt her arch her shoulders, push her breast up for him to take more. "Ah . . . oooh, oh, yes," Vera breathed, and he felt her stiffen for an instant as he began to trace a candent path with his lips across both full breasts, down along her abdomen, moved back and forth over her deep belly button and down over her convex little belly. Vera's breathy cries had become an almost continuous moaning murmur, and when he let his fingers push through the dark, curly tuft, he felt her hands dig into his back. "Oh, Fargo, oh, God," she cried out.

He moved down, slowly, let his hand rest at the very opening of the dark, warm portal, slowly pressed his palm against the softness there, and Vera half-screamed in anxious delight. He moved his hand, began to gently stroke the lubricious lips, and saw her thighs fall open and close, fall open again and half-twist, close, and return to open again. "Oh, God, oh, oh, God, so good, oh, my, oh, my," Vera gasped out as he probed deeper into the dark warmth, and her cries became small screams.

He felt her hands moving up and down his back, along his body, pulling him to her, pressing, each motion a silent exhortation of the flesh. He caressed deeper, and her cries grew stronger as her hands began to almost fly up and down his back, grasping, pulling away, pressing, rubbing. Vera's rounded hips moved sideways, half-twisting as he pressed deeper, and he could feel the fear mixed in with the desire as she pushed against him, then pulled him to her. He moved his body over hers, pressed his hot, pulsating organ against the fleshy little pubic mound, and Vera cried out, a sharp cry of fear again, then the instant wanting as she pushed up against him.

"Fargo, oh, my God, oh, please . . . oh, please, please," she gasped.

"Please what?" he murmured as he pressed his face into the rounded cups of her breasts.

"I don't know. I don't know," Vera half-shouted. "Oh, God, I don't know. Please, please, God, whatever, please."

His smile was buried against one tiny pink nipple that had grown firm, and he lifted, pushed into the steaming warmth of her, and she screamed, the eternal scream of discovery and desire. "Oh, oh, oooaaee," Vera groaned. He moved slowly, felt the tightness of her around him, and her fleshy thighs fell open again. She pushed up, offering the warm path for his taking. He moved deeper and she cried out, a brief moment of pain, and he halted, rested. "No . . . no. Go on, go on," Vera cried out, and he slid forward and her groan seemed to come from deep in her abdomen, consuming, enveloping, ecstasy and release, abandon and acceptance.

He began to move slowly inside her, the warm passage moist, especially slowly, and he felt her responding with heightening desire, each breath a long, gasping cry. He resisted the impulse to quicken his movements, held his own desire back, and continued the tantalizing slowness of each thrust until he began to feel her legs lift, her thighs tighten against him. "Oh, my God, oh, Fargo . . . oh, oh, my God . . . aaaa . . . eeee . . . iiiiiii," Vera cried out, gasped, half-screamed, and her full breasts lifted, quivered, and she contracted around him, flowed, and grew rigid as her climax swept through her. Her scream buried itself against his chest as she clung to him, and he heard her half-sobbing, half-laughing cry that finally trailed away into a groan of protest. "Oh, no . . . no, oh, God, oh, more, more," she breathed against him as he sank back with her, stayed inside her as she slowly shuddered herself still.

Her round eyes opened to stare at him as if she were seeing for the first time. He cupped one round breast in his hand as he slowly slid from her and lay half atop her rounded little belly. Her lips opened against his. "Thank you," she breathed, but he put a finger against her mouth. "I thought I'd be ready," she said. "But I wasn't."

"You never are, especially the first time," he told her.

He saw the newfound womanly slyness come into

her little smile. "Will there be a second time?" she asked.

"Could be," he said.

"Not tonight," she said quickly. "I want to take it all in again alone, sort of let everything curl up inside me. Is that being silly?"

"No," he told her, and kissed the round, soft breasts. He rose, started to pull on clothes, and she clasped her arms around his waist, rested her head against his hard, flat abdomen.

"I was right in picking you. I knew you'd understand. I knew," Vera said.

He lifted her to her feet and patted her round little rear. "Was it everything you expected?" he asked.

She nodded vigorously. "You made it that. I know that much," she said.

"Get some sleep," he told her as he finished dressing and climbed from the tailgate of the wagon. He strolled slowly back to the other campsite, his eyes sweeping the area out of habit. Nothing moved, but he noted that the captain hadn't set out sentries. He grunted. Petty stubbornness or an attempt to show independent authority? Either one spelled stupid, he muttered silently as he took his bedroll and carried it to the side of the camp.

But the night stayed quiet, and he soon fell asleep, waking with the new sun. He rose, washed, and saddled the Ovaro as the others stirred. The troopers were quickly ready to ride, and Fargo saw Blossom come toward him, the very blue eyes very icy.

"You'd no need to go chasing over there last night," she said.

"Didn't go chasing. I was invited," Fargo said.

"And you just can't resist a piece of tail," Blossom snapped.

"You're sot of jumping to conclusions, aren't you?" he returned.

"I might be with somebody else, not with you," Blossom hissed.

"Didn't figure you for the jealous type," Fargo commented mildly, and Blossom's eyes hardened.

"I'm not jealous, damn you. I just don't want you getting too chummy over there. I'm not paying you to wet-nurse those fools," Blossom bit out.

"You're all heart, aren't you, Blossom?" Fargo said.

"Go to hell," she threw back, and stalked away. His laugh followed her as he swung onto the Ovaro. He saw Yuma take to the saddle as Senator Talbot walked by, his face tight. He threw Fargo an angry glance as he hurried toward the troopers. Olive Reamer followed in the tailored brown riding outfit and nodded pleasantly.

"What's eating him so early in the day?" Fargo asked, and gestured toward the senator.

"He's upset. The senator is becoming convinced you're taking us out of our way just to give those settlers protection," the woman said.

"You think that too?" Fargo asked her calmly.

Her little smile was filled with private amusement. "No, I don't think that," Olive Reamer said. "But I think you're up to something."

He laughed as his original estimate of her was reinforced—she had proved again to be the cleverest of the lot. He sent the Ovaro into a trot and headed away from the campsite as Capt. Ellwood ordered his troops to mount. He glanced back to see the three wagons starting to roll, and he rode on as Yuma caught up to him. The older man pointed a knobby elbowed arm at a line of hoofprints to the right, and Fargo nodded as he swung his horse to the left and Yuma turned right. They rode double point, trotted beyond sight of the column, and Fargo saw that the unshod hoofprints grew more plentiful.

It was just past the noon hour when he cut back to

where Yuma had halted. "Make anything out of it?" Fargo asked as Yuma's eyes studied the line of hoofprints.

"Mostly small hunting parties," Yuma said. "We'll have to get closer."

Fargo gestured to the horizon where the foothills of the Sacramento Mountains were barely visible through the shimmering haze of the burning sun. "We'll be close enough by nightfall," he said as he dismounted and let the Ovaro graze on a patch of dropseed grass. The column rode up a few minutes later, Blossom alongside the captain, the senator and Olive behind, with Robertson and Downs at their heels. The senator perspired heavily, Fargo noted, his face florid, while Olive Reamer seemed absolutely cool. The captain swung from his mount and cast a glance back to where the three wagons rolled steadily on.

"Those damn settlers are still following us," he growled angrily.

"That any skin off your back?" Fargo asked.

"I told them no escort. I don't like being used," the captain snapped.

"You don't like being outsmarted." Fargo grinned, swung up on the Ovaro, and rode away. Yuma came after him, changed direction, and rode point to the northeast. As the day wore down and they neared the mountain range; the grama grass began to grow more thickly and the soil took on moisture. The sun had started to dip over the horizon as Fargo drew up before the foothills of the mountains the Americans called the Sacramento Mountains and the Spaniards had called the Guadalupe. No thick, lush range of greenery such as the Rockies, they were largely rock, with a thin covering of heavy brush, some oak, cottonwood, hawthorn and Douglas fir. But the Sacramento Mountains were filled with passages, arroyos, unexpected mountain glens, and flat plains, mountains made for hiding and ambushing.

Fargo drew up along the rise of the foothills, a circular area large enough to make camp, and he dismounted as the lavender of dusk rolled across the land. Yuma rode to a halt and swung down from his quarter horse, grimness in every line of his weathered face. "Plenty of tracks, plenty of Mescalero," he grunted. "Got a camp somewhere not too far up in the mountains."

"What makes you think so?" Fargo questioned.

"Lots of small hunting parties scouting around for game, crossing back and forth," Yuma said.

Fargo's eyes moved to the mountains beyond the foothills, and he squinted in the last dim light. The wide passageway rose slowly through the foothills, and when he turned back to Yuma, his mouth was a tight line. The column led by Capt. Ellwood and Blossom rode up and filed off against the rocks. In the distance, Fargo glimpsed the dark bulk of the three wagons slowly moving toward the foothills. The captain helped Blossom from her horse as the senator and the others rode up and dismounted. The senator's face still wore anger, and Fargo watched as the man strode toward him, the others following. The captain moved up from the side as the senator halted to glare at him. Fargo waited, his face expressionless.

"We decided it was time for a meeting, Fargo," the senator barked.

"We?" Fargo asked.

"The captain and I, we talked about it," the senator said, and Fargo's eyes went to Blossom. She half-shrugged almost apologetically.

"I'm wondering myself, Fargo," she said.

"We're all wondering if you've come this way just to do those settlers a backhanded favor," the senator snapped.

"Frankly, Fargo, I don't share Major Carpenter's confidence in your integrity," Capt. Ellwood sniffed.

"I'm all upset about that," Fargo said.

"Well, do you have any good reason for bringing us up here after the Mescalero instead of the Jicarilla or the Chiricahua?" the senator demanded.

Fargo reached into his jacket pocket and pulled out the torn piece of calfskin. He tossed it at the senator's feet, and Olive Reamer was quickest to pick it up.

"There's my reason," Fargo said.

"This is a piece of moccasin," Olive said as she held the torn length of calfskin in her hand. "What does it mean?"

"It means the Apache who took Dale Talbot were Mescalero," Fargo snapped. "This belonged to one of them. The guide that was with him picked it up afterward."

"Why'd you hold back on this?" the captain asked as he took the piece of moccasin from Olive's hand.

"Didn't want to see you go running off half-cocked," Fargo replied mildly.

"And leave those wagons behind," the captain said.

"You're just full of suspicions," Fargo said.

"No matter," the captain answered. "This settles our next move—capture and interrogate."

"Nothin' to it," Yuma commented.

Capt. Ellwood ignored Yuma's remark and focused his attention on the big man standing by. "I'll send two troopers to scout with you in the morning," he said.

"I scout alone," Fargo said flatly, and turned away at once, the gesture cutting off any further discussion.

"Rations are ready," the sergeant called, and the others started to drift over to where the troopers were already lined up for rations.

Fargo waited till the last one had helped himself, then took a plate of beans and beef jerky, sat down

94

alone, and looked up as Robertson and Downs came to sit nearby.

"Your client, Miss Daley, seems an interesting young woman," Robertson said. "She must have very deep feelings for Dale Talbot to come way out here on her own to try to find him."

"Guess so," Fargo agreed pleasantly.

"She tell you anything else about herself?" Downs asked too casually.

"Not a damn thing," Fargo answered with matching casualness. "You curious about her, why not ask her yourselves?"

"That wouldn't be polite," Robertson said. "Besides, it's just idle curiosity on our part." He smiled and rose to his feet, Downs following at once. "Good night, Fargo," Robertson said, and the two men returned their plates to the troop sergeant.

Idle curiosity, my ass, Fargo thought as he finished the meal, returned his plate, and saw the senator and Capt. Ellwood in earnest conversation. Blossom, off to one side, glanced at him as she prepared her blanket, and he nodded at Yuma as he passed and started to walk from the campsite. He slowed as Olive Reamer appeared, a faint smile on her lips as she studied him appraisingly, her heavy breasts straining the lines of the tailored riding jacket. "Going visiting again?" she asked.

"Why not?" He shrugged.

"I'm wondering if it's just that girl over there," Olive Reamer said.

"Got a better reason for me not to go?" he asked.

Her eyes narrowed at him. "Would you stay if I gave you one?" she asked.

"You asking or offering?" he returned.

She paused for a moment. "Offering," she said softly.

His eyes went over Olive Reamer's full, womanly

shape, took in the contained, mature sensuousness she held to herself. "When and where?" he said.

"When the others go to sleep. I'm sure you can find where on a warm night like this," she answered.

"I'm sure," he said, nodded, and turned away and strolled back into the campsite to settle down against a slab of stone. He laughed silently. Not visiting the wagons wouldn't make a damn bit of difference, but Olive didn't know that, of course. He wasn't about to tell her either.

He let himself speculate on the woman as he relaxed. She'd been quick to take up his challenge, and he'd know soon enough if the thoughts that danced through his mind were right. He put his head back and let himself half-doze as the camp fell into slumber. Blossom slept heavily to one side, he saw, and the others were all hard asleep as Olive appeared, came toward him on slippered feet, a dark-green full-lenth robe pulled tight around her. He waited till she reached him, and then he turned and began to move up into the nearest hillside. Olive fell into step beside him as he led the way in silence.

The campsite had disappeared below in the darkness when he found a small alcove of rock and two twisted burr oaks with a bed of thick white cushion moss. He halted and his eyes swept the hills nearby.

"Something wrong?" Olive asked.

"No," he said, returning his eyes to her. "But if the captain doesn't start posting sentries, you won't be around to find Dale Talbot." He sank down on the moss and Olive dropped to her knees beside him.

"I'll have the senator insist on it in the morning," she said.

"You pretty chummy with the senator?" Fargo asked, leaning on one elbow.

"Depends on what you mean by chummy," Olive Reamer said as she stayed on her knees, her hands

96

resting on the front of her legs. "You pretty chummy with that girl in the wagon train?" she asked.

"Depends on what you mean by chummy." He smiled.

Olive's laugh was low, throaty. "I like you, Fargo," she said. "You're going to be trouble, I know it, but I like you." Her hand went to the belt of the robe that tightly encased her body. "And I didn't come up here to spar with you," she said as she pulled the belt free. The robe fell open and Fargo watched the heavy breasts spill out, tremendous white mounds that made the brown-pink nipples seem tinier than they actually were, the pink circles around each full and large. Olive shrugged her shoulders and the robe fell from her, and he saw a fleshy belly, full, wide hips amply covered, a wide rib cage, and a dark, curly triangle that narrowed to a V where full-fleshed thighs curved downward. Olive Reamer carried perhaps fifteen pounds too many, but it was evenly distributed over her body, a body still ripe, skin still smooth and firm, the body of a woman in the full flush of her maturity. He pulled his clothes off quickly and heard her intake of breath as he rose with his hard-muscled nakedness before her.

"Come on, oh, Jesus, come on," Olive Reamer breathed as he sank to his knees. She fell against him, and he let himself topple back and felt the heavy breasts sink down over his face, almost smothering as they enveloped him with their blanketing softness. She rubbed her breasts back and forth across his face, brought one hand up, and guided her right breast into his mouth. His lips pressed down and he heard her guttural rasp of breath as he pulled on the firm brown-pink tip, letting his teeth sink gently into the pillowed softness. He felt her thighs over him, moving apart, pressing down, and his hands clasped around the heavy buttocks that rose up as her body seemed to grope for him. "Fargo, Jesus, take me, oh, Christ," Olive Reamer breathed, her voice low, a deep rasped sound, and her raw, enveloping excitement swept over him as she rubbed and pressed, rose and fell back against him.

He pushed, turned, flung her onto her back even as he kept his hold on one heavy breast, biting down a fraction harder than he'd intended, but her hoarse cry was one of pleasure. He felt the fleshy folds of her convex belly pressed up against him and heard her harsh, deep breaths. His probing, seeking maleness found her, touched her waiting, wanting portal, and felt the wet warmth of her at once. Olive Reamer's hands clasped against his back and she pulled hard as she gasped pleas in a voice that had dropped still lower. "Ah . . . ah, go on, go on . . . Christ, go on, oh, Jesus," she rasped, and he drew up, plunged hard, and felt the lubricious passageway welcome him with wet, warm width. "Aaaah . . . aaaaggggh . . ." Olive cried out, and her voice continued to grow deeper as he worked inside her with long, hard-thrusting plunges. Her hands came underneath the heavy breasts as they fell to her sides, gathered their softness up, and pushed it at him, and he plunged his face into their pillowed mass. He plunged harder, deeper, and her groans of pleasure became half-roars. Her fleshy thighs locked around his buttocks, spread down over his steel-muscled legs, like a pillowed vise.

In the midst of passion, the thought, like an errant flicker of flame, flared in his mind: Olive Reamer wanted him with a raw, throbbing hunger, no matter what other reasons had brought her to him. That question was answered by her grasping, heaving ecstasy as she rose up under him, lifted, and he heard her groans become a guttural breath. He felt her body begin to shake, the heavy breasts quivering almost jellylike, and her hand clutched at him, dug into his back. "Ahh

. . . aaaagh . . . ah, Christ, now, now, I'm coming, oh, Jesus, Jesus . . . aaaaggghhhh," Olive moaned the low, rasping sound rising to become a full-throated roar that seemed to tear itself from her very depths. Her heavy thighs tightened hard against him, and he felt himsef explode with her as she shook, quivered, convulsed, and finally, with an anguished groan, fell back on the soft moss to lay panting heavily, the big breasts heaving up and down with each harsh breath.

He lowered his head against their flaccid softness and she cradled his face against her at once, held him there until her heaving breath returned to normal. "Jesus," Olive muttered through another gasped breath, and he lifted his head to look down at her. She grasped his hand, pressed it against her wet, warm triangle, and held it there as ner fleshy belly slowed its quivering. "It helps me slow down," she said to him as she kept his hand against her.

"My pleasure." Fargo smiled. "You don't hold back any, do you?"

"No reason to when you get to be my age," she said. "I don't get that many chances with somebody such as you." She pushed herself up on her elbows, and the heavy breasts fell to one side to press against his chest. "Whenever and wherever you want, Fargo," she murmured.

"You telling me something, Olive?" He grinned.

The contained little smile touched her lips and she rubbed her breasts against him. "I'm telling you there's no need to go off to those wagons to enjoy yourself."

"Guess not." He smiled and pushed himself to his feet as he reached for his trousers. "We'd best get you back before somebody wakes up."

Olive nodded, rose, and wrapped her full-fleshed form around him for another moment. "You enjoy yourself, Fargo?" she asked.

"Every minute of it," he told her, and meant his words. He dressed quickly and Olive wrapped the robe tightly around her once again. She was silent during the walk back down the hillside to the camp as Fargo's eyes swept the surrounding crags. When they reached the campsite, he let her go in alone, worked his way around the edges of the semicircle to come in from the other side. Olive's last quick glance at him had carried more than satisfaction in it. An edge of triumph had been in her eyes, and he smiled as he settled onto his bedroll to sleep until the morning finally came.

He woke to see the sun a hazy sphere over the mountains. He dressed, moved up to the far side of the campsite, and waited till the others were up and dressed before walking back down again.

Capt. Ellwood strolled over to the senator and Olive with tin mugs of coffee, and Fargo saw Blossom still combing her blond hair. Yuma moved closer, his weathered face holding quiet amusement in it. Fargo halted before Sen. Talbot, Capt. Ellwood, and Olive as Robertson and Downs appeared. Both fully dressed, they looked as if they were going to an office rather than riding trail.

"Got a few things to say this morning," Fargo announced, and saw Blossom lower her comb to listen. He focused his gaze on the captain. "The folks in those wagons have to take the passage through the mountains that cuts right through Mescalero country," Fargo began. "They might not make it anyway, but they'll sure as hell never make it on their own. I'm going to try to get them through."

"You're going to do what?" The captain frowned.

"I'm going to do what's right. I'm going to do what you ought to be doing," Fargo returned, his voice growing hard.

"I told you I'm not obliged to give them an escort," Capt. Ellwood snapped.

"You're not obliged to give the senator one either," Fargo tossed back. "Because you want to play up to him, you're sending three wagons of settlers to their deaths. You're abandoning them."

The senator's angry voice cut in. "And you're abandoning my brother because you want to play hero for those damn fools. That doesn't make you any better than the captain," he roared.

"Try again," Fargo snapped. "Dale Talbot's either long dead or he's being held as a slave. If he's dead, time doesn't mean anything to him. If they're keeping him as a slave, he'll still be alive a week from now. You've nothing to lose, but those people have their lives on the line."

"I remind you, Fargo, that you've been paid and hired to help find Dale Talbot," the captain said stiffly.

"By me, too," Blossom put in. "You can't just walk out on me."

"I'll be back," Fargo said.

"You were hired to stay on till we find this man. I insist on nothing less," the captain ordered.

"Me, too," Blossom added.

"I brought you this far, told you the Mescalero took him. I figure I've earned my hire. Now I'm going to do what's right. You don't want to wait till I get back, that's your problem," Fargo said.

"You can't, dammit," Blossom shouted. "I paid you to help me. I don't give a damn about those fools back there."

"Tough shit, honey," Fargo said, as he turned away.

"It's all right, Blossom. I'm quite capable of finding Dale Talbot for everyone concerned," the captain answered.

"Oh, shut up," Fargo heard Blossom snap as she stalked away. He laughed softly as he walked to the

Ovaro. He'd just finished tightening the rigging straps under the horse when Olive halted beside him, her eyes narrowed as she studied his face.

"You planned all this back at the post. That's why they've been following us. You knew that last night," Olive said. "I underestimated you."

"No, you overestimated last night," Fargo said.

A faint smile touched the corners of her mouth. "It seems so. But it was still great," she said.

"Good." Fargo smiled.

"You know, the captain may find Dale Talbot for us and surprise you," Olive said.

"Surprise will be the right word," Fargo said, and swung onto the Ovaro. He nodded to Olive and put the horse into a trot as he headed for the distant, waiting wagons.

Yuma crossed from one side to join him as he reached the wagons. The others were all standing beside their wagons, Jeb White in the forefront and Ned Snyder, a fresh bandage still covering the wound on his bald pate, alongside Jeb. Fargo saw Vera's round eyes follow him from the last wagon, and she gave a little wave with one hand, an almost shy motion.

"We're all mighty grateful to you and Mister Kelly for what you're doing," Jeb said.

"You can be grateful after you make it through," Fargo said curtly. "Let's roll." As everyone climbed into their wagons, he paused beside Vera. Four youngsters, excitement in their faces, rode with her.

"Kept hoping you'd stop by last night," Vera said as she snapped the reins. No protest or complaint in her voice, he noted, yet it was more than a comment, an edge of disappointment in it.

"Didn't work out," he said. "Want me to stop by tonight?"

"Please," Vera said with a quick rush of breath.

He pressed her arm for a moment and then sent the Ovaro into a fast trot. Yuma fell in beside him as he headed for the wide passage that rose slowly up into the mountains. They had just reached the start of it when he caught the flash of yellow and saw the big gray horse hurrying toward him. He halted as Blossom reined up, a half-pout on her face.

"Good luck," she said almost crossly, and he waited. "I didn't mean what I said before, about not giving a damn about those people. You're right to help them," she said.

He let a slow smile reach out to her. "Glad to see you're only hard-nosed, not hardhearted," he said.

"Hurry back, please," Blossom said with a note of desperation in her voice. "I want you to find Dale first, for me."

"Why?" Fargo tossed at her.

She hesitated only a fraction of a second. "I'm the only one who really cares about him," she answered, and Fargo nodded as she wheeled the big grey and rode away. He watched her go, his eyes lingering on the extra pack still firmly on the horse's rump.

"There's a girl who's bent on being stupid," Fargo said.

"And still trying to con you," Yuma said. "She and all the others. Sure makes me wonder why they're really so all fired anxious to find this Dale Talbot."

"We'll answer that when we get back," Fargo said.

"Let's ride. I hate to keep the Mescalero waiting," Yuma said, and drew a glance from the big man beside him. "Makes 'em mad," Yuma added.

5

The wide passageway narrowed slightly as it rose higher into the mountains, but it stayed at a slow incline the wagons could easily handle. Unshod pony tracks became too common to read as the day wore on, and twice Fargo saw the thin spiral of dust from below that marked the captain leading the column on a sweep through the lower passages. Fargo rode at one edge of the passage, Yuma at the other side, and they constantly surveyed the crags and tree cover on the high land on both sides of the trail.

As day began to near an end, Fargo spotted a place that branched off from the passage to become a flat square of land large enough to hold the three wagons. He had a small fire started as the wagons rolled up and formed a half-circle in the square.

"We made good time today," Jeb White said as the dark fell and the others gathered around the fire. Two of the women acted as cooks, Fargo saw, and he glimpsed Vera as she shepherded the four youngsters back to their folks.

"Didn't see any Mescalero," Jeb commented.

"You won't see them till they want you to see them," Yuma answered. "Leastwise not up here."

Vera came to sit beside Fargo with her plate, and when the meal ended, she took his plate back to clean it with hers. Fargo rose as others began to douse the fire. "Sentries," he said to Jeb. "Two will do here. Four hours each man."

Jeb nodded and proceeded to assign men and shifts as Fargo settled himself in a corner of the half-circle. He waited, let sleep take over the camp, and undressed to his trousers before making his way to Vera's wagon. She pulled the back flap open as he reached it, and a tiny candle inside a tin cup gave off just enough wavering light for him to see that she wore a loose, filmy nightgown that rested lightly against the tips of her full, high breasts. Her brown eyes, round as saucers, stayed on him as he sat down before her on a blanket folded over the floor of the wagon.

"Thanks for coming, Fargo," she said. "I didn't realize something."

"Such as?" he asked, and enjoyed the tiny point that thrust against the filmy material as she moved.

Her eyes stayed round and grave. "It's sort of like having ice cream for the first time, isn't it?" she said. "Once you have it, you want it again."

"Sort of like that." He laughed.

"I'm being bold as brass again," she said apologetically.

"You're being honest again," he told her.

She leaned forward earnestly and her breasts pressed into the nightgown, drawing the thin material around each. "If you don't want to, I'll understand. It likely wasn't much for you last time," she said.

"It was fine," he said.

"You don't have to say that," she began, and he pressed her lips silent with his.

"Stop your chatter," he said, and closed his hand around one full, firm breast, cupping it through the thin nightgown, and Vera squealed. He drew back, pushed trousers off as Vera lifted the nightgown over her head and cast it aside. Her firm breasts seemed to beckon, her rounded little body vibrant with that combination of innocence and sensuousness that was hers. He moved to her and felt his eager organ spring up, not unlike a jack-in-the-box released, as he tore off underwear. It came against Vera's abdomen with a tiny slapping sound and she gasped out a short, breath-filled cry.

"Oh, my goodness . . . oh, Fargo," she swallowed, and he pressed her down on the blanket, lowered his body atop her, and felt the wonderfully warm, tactile pleasure of her soft roundness against him. She clasped his face to hers, arms around his neck. "I've been burning up since the other night," she whispered into his ear. "Maybe it was wrong to do it. Maybe I should never have."

"You're chattering again," he said as he rubbed both hands over her firm breasts, and she trembled with pleasure. Her lips, warm with wanting, found his, and he felt her tongue sliding out, desire its own tutor. He let his hands rove over her vibrant firmness, traced little lines of sensuous flame over hips, belly, up to the high, breasts, around each pink circle, and down over her abdomen to pause at the dark indentation in the center of her belly. Vera's firm-fleshed young legs moved, her knees lifting, stretching out, lifting again, and her thighs falling open as his fingers pushed through the dark, wire-nap triangle to the soft tip of her quivering, moist lips.

"Fargo, Fargo, yes, yes . . . please, please," she called out as her head turned from side to side and her hands became little fists that beat against his shoulders. He touched, pressed, parted the aqueous lips, and Vera's cry trailed off in the air in a long, breathless gasp. He moved, brought his pulsating maleness to her, slid slowly into her, and she moaned and pulled his mouth down to her breasts. She glided with him, her torso moving smoothly with each of his gentle thrusts, as though, he found himself thinking, she'd been doing it for years. Wanting and pleasure were teachers that ignored time, he thought, and smiled as he increased his forward motions.

He felt Vera brace herself as the spiral began to wind up inside her and her gasps began to lift from her lips in tiny puffs of air. "Fargo, Fargo . . . oh, oh, oh . . . oh, God, oh . . ." she cried out, and suddenly her high breasts were pressed hard against him, her rounded little body wrapped around him almost with desperation. Her head fell back as the cry erupted from her lips, and he felt her belly trembling violently against him as she gave herself to the climax of ecstasy.

When the hanging moment ended and she fell from him, her arms stayed around his neck, pulling him down atop her. "Stay with me, Fargo," she breathed against him. "Stay with me." He lay his lips against one light-pink nipple in answer as he settled down beside her.

She slept against him until he rose as the dawn tinted the sky and filtered through the canvas of the wagon. The sight of her sweet sensuality stayed with him as he hurried outside to his bedroll and dressed quickly. He was first to take a mug of coffee from a pleasant-faced woman in the second wagon, and he watched the sun burn through haze again. Yuma came up as his eyes scanned the sky.

"There's bad weather on the way," Fargo said.

"Seems so," Yuma agreed, and walked with him to gaze up along the passageway into the mountains.

"This go all the way through?" Fargo asked.

"It crests midway up and gets a lot steeper, but it's the only passage that cuts directly through," Yuma said.

Fargo turned back to the semicircle as the camp came awake and he smiled at the shining in Vera's eyes as she emerged from the wagon. Yuma followed him as he took the pinto out onto the passageway and began to ride on. He rode slowly, taking in the silence that seemed to blanket the mountains.

"Too quiet," Yuma grunted, picking up on Fargo's uneasiness, and the big man nodded. It was mid-morning when they halted and let the wagons roll up to rest the horses. Fargo pointed below to the thin spiral of dust that rose up, farther to the west this time.

"Captain Ellwood's column again?" Jeb White asked, and Fargo's eyes were narrowed as he nodded. "Wonder if he's seen any more Mescalero than we have," Jeb said.

"I'd guess so," Yuma answered. "They're likely leading him away from the camp they have down there."

"I think we owe the captain a vote of thanks," Fargo said, and drew a questioning glance from Jeb and Zach Diamond. "I figure he's giving us two free days," Fargo explained. "The Mescalero are watching us and they're watching him. Right now they're not sure whether we've been set up as a decoy or a trap, so they're hanging back, testing the captain's troopers. Soon as they decide that we're on our own, they'll come for us." His eyes swept the grave faces that listened, paused at Vera, and saw her try to look hopeful. "I want to be at the crest by then, so they'll have to come up at us," Fargo said.

Yuma made a face. "Not likely," he said. "We'll need a few more days than they're going to give us to make the crest. Better figure on making a stand before then."

"When the time comes," Fargo said. "Meanwhile, let's keep rolling." He sent the Ovaro up the path as the wagons began to move again and the thick haze over the sun made the air heavy with dampness. He called more frequent halts to rest the horses, and at one stop he circled back to Vera's wagon. Her dark-tan shirt had grown wet with perspiration to outline the firm breasts with tantalizing clarity. She saw his glance and he caught the little smile of pride that touched her lips.

"You wouldn't have smiled a week back," he told her.

"That's right. I'd have been embarrassed," she agreed. "It's called growing up."

He laughed and spurred the Ovaro forward again to swing in beside Yuma as he rode point. The passage began to grow steeper and the sun stayed behind the curtain of thick haze. Fargo's lips pulled back in distaste. The storms that came through the mountains erupted out of the tremendous buildup of heat and the rain clouds pulled down to bring violent winds and awesome lightning. "We've another twenty-four hours, I'd guess," he muttered to Yuma as he swept the sky again with narrowed eyes. He kept a steady pace until the night slid down the high crags and he found a place to camp alongside a cluster of high-branched Douglas firs.

Jeb White sat with him as they ate, and Fargo held back answers while the man's hope bubbled over.

"We're making good time. We haven't seen a Mescalero, in spite of what Yuma said. I'm feeling good about it," Jeb said.

"Keep the faith," Fargo grunted.

"If we have trouble, every one of the women can handle a rifle," Jeb told him.

"Good," Fargo said, not ungratefully.

"Could be that Captain Ellwood's keeping them busy down below," Jeb reflected.

"Could be," Fargo said, but he knew that, if anything, the truth was exactly opposite. Despite his beliefs, he let Jeb White turn in for the night with his hopes intact.

The camp settled down to sleep and Jeb posted sentries at each end of the cluster of firs. Fargo stayed on his bedroll, then undressed to his trousers and made his way to Vera's wagon in the inky blackness of a moonless night. The little candle in the wagon had burned itself out, but he needed no light to find her firm, young nakedness. She pressed herself hard against him, and the warmth of her was instantly exciting. He sank down on the blanket with her, holding her to him. Vera had been more than a surprise. She had been a touching, endearing interlude as she tried to encompass the world in a few nights, fearing that there would be no tomorrows. She lay against him, her firm, sweet young body delicious to the touch.

"Could be the last night for a spell," he told her gently.

"Then we'll make it special," she murmured as her hand pulled his belt open and stole down into his trousers. He heard her sharp cry of delight as her fingers closed around him. She moved quickly to make her promise come true, and the night became clothed in pure physical enjoyment until finally she slept in his arms, spent and satiated. He pulled on his trousers and stole away from the wagon with the new day.

He finished dressing quickly and the sky was a gray haze as he rode the Ovaro out onto the passage. He climbed the path and Yuma caught up to him later when he halted, his gaze sweeping the heavy sky. The passage suddenly grew steep and Fargo felt the hot wind blow over him in quick spurts, fade away, and then blow again.

"Heavy weather by night," he muttered to Yuma, and waited until the wagons rolled up. He pulled the Ovaro to one side and watched the horses dig deep into the soil where the path grew steep. Satisfied they could negotiate the incline, he rode on and halted again where the passage almost leveled off onto a high plateau. Another burst of hot wind flung itself into his face and the gray sky grew grayer. The wagons rolled up and he waved them on without rest, his eyes sweeping the crags above unceasingly.

By midafternoon the mountains were still too quiet, Fargo thought, not even a horned lizard showing itself. His lips pulled back in distaste, knowing all too well the meaning of the silence. The passage began to rise again and Fargo held a steady pace, staying just ahead of the wagons, and suddenly, as if by magic, the line of figures appeared on the rocks above.

Fargo raised his arm and the wagons came to a halt behind him as he looked up at the line of figures that stood silent and still as wood carvings against the gray sky. He counted ten, each on horseback. A few were bare-chested, wearing only knee-length pants, but most wore long-sleeved white tunics with belts of rawhide tied at the waist. All wore the long, stringy, almost-shoulder-length black hair and brow bands that was the trademark of the Mescalero. One held a long lance, the others short bows, and as Fargo watched, the one with the lance turned his pony and the others followed as if they were one. The Mescalero began to slowly move down from the high rocks, single-file, threading their way through the narrow passageways among the rocks. Fargo glanced at the wagons, and saw everyone but the children with a rifle in hand, faces tense with fear. Vera held a big, old Hawken, he noted. He put calmness into his voice.

"No shooting. Stay cool," he said. "There are probably another ten out of sight up in the rocks."

"Why are they coming down?" Zach Diamond asked.

"To have a closer look at us and to try their hand at bargaining, their kind of bargaining," Fargo answered.

The line of Apache disappeared behind the rocks for a moment, and when they came into sight again, they were directly in front of them on the passageway.

They formed a line blocking the wagons' path as the one with the lance detached himself from the others and moved his pony forward.

Fargo moved the Ovaro forward to meet him half-way. He unholstered the Colt as he did so and let the gun hang down from his right hand. The Indian halted and slid from his pony, the lance firmly in one hand. Fargo halted and dismounted, faced the Apache across a dozen or so feet of the path.

The face under the dark-red brow band was typically Apache, he saw: broad, flattened features and small, narrowed eyes. But the right corner of the Indian's mouth pulled downward to give him a perpetual half-snarl. His little eyes glittered as he peered at the big man, and he flung words in clusters, contempt and hate coating each one. "Horses, wagons," the Apache barked. "Horses, wagons, you go free."

Fargo's smile was made of ice. "We cross mountains in peace," he said.

"Horses, wagons," the Indian repeated adamantly.

Fargo shook his head. It was a game, but there were rules and he had to go with them. "No horses. No wagons. We go on," he said.

The Apache's black eyes grew harder, sharper. "Horses, wagons, you go alive," he tossed back, and there was more anger in his voice.

Fargo shook his head again.

"No horses, no wagons, you die," the Mescalero said, his voice rising.

"No. We go on," Fargo said evenly.

The Indian's eyes flared and the corner of his mouth seemed to pull down still further. "Horses, wagons, you go alive," he said again, and once more Fargo shook his head.

He heard the Apache's hiss of anger as the Indian raised the lance. Fargo watched it hurtle through the air to embed itself in the ground an inch from his foot.

He didn't move as it quivered there in front of him. Not just an angry gesture, he realized, but a final statement, demands repeated one more time with unmistakable emphasis. The Mescalero's eyes bored into him, waiting.

Fargo raised the Colt and fired, a single shot. It sent a spray of dirt up an inch from the Apache's foot. The man didn't move, his eyes black ice. But he understood. His statement had been answered in kind. Finally, he turned, pulled himself onto his pony, and slowly rode back to the others.

Fargo watched as they fell in behind him in single file and made their way back up the narrow mountain passes to the high ground. When the Apache disappeared from view, he turned to the wagons and swept the anxious, tense faces with a glance of grim humor.

"Not too neighborly a chat," Fargo commented.

"What if we gave them the horses and wagons?" a woman asked. "We'd still have our lives."

"Not for long," Fargo grunted.

"They wouldn't keep their word?" Zach frowned.

"Not to you. You've got to understand the Apache, especially the Mescalero. Words to white men are meant to be broken. They have nothing but contempt and hate for you," Fargo explained.

"Why they'd try to bargain us out of the horses and wagons, then?" Jeb asked.

"The Apache always make things as easy as they can for themselves. Without horses and wagons you'd be sitting ducks," Fargo said.

"Then they'll be attacking us now," Zach said.

Fargo's glance went to the thick gray of the sky, and a gust of wind swirled around him as if in answer to his thoughts. "Not with that storm ready to hit. I figure it'll hit in full force in about an hour. They're on their way to hole up till it's over, come morning. They'll figure that'll be the perfect time to strike." He paused,

113

swept the others with his eyes grown hard. "But we won't be waiting," he said, and drew questioning stares. "We're going to move through the storm," he said, and heard the almost concerted gasp.

"Through the storm?" Jeb White echoed. "Across the mountain? Impossible."

"Nothing's impossible, and we've got to make it," Fargo said. "It's our only chance not to be massacred. It'll give us another six to eight hours." His eyes went to Yuma, and the older man nodded as his lips pursed in thought.

"Just about enough time to make the crest," Yuma said. "They'll have to come up at us there. It's our one place to make a stand. But we have to reach it."

Fargo let a grim sound escape his lips as he swept the wagons with a hard glance. "We'll roll for another half-hour and I'll spell out the rest then."

A gust of wind swirled around him and he felt a few drops of rain. The wind blew harder and then whirled away as if the heavens were mocking his temerity. He headed the Ovaro upward and heard the wagons begin to roll after him. He found a stand of hackberry that offered shelter, and pulled into it as a flash of lightning crackled across the mountains. He dismounted as the wagons rolled into a half-circle and he watched Jeb and the others step out, their eyes grave, their faces filled with apprehension. A sudden gust of rain swept down through the trees—no mockery, this time, a challenge flung down.

Jeb White's eyes went to the quivering trees for an instant and returned to the big man. "We're afraid, Fargo," he said.

"You should be," Fargo said. "But think about the Mescalero. They're certain death." He watched as Jeb's grim nod answered for everyone. "Get all your heavy-rain gear on, men, women, and children. Everybody walks." He saw the collective frown

114

appear, and his words were terse. "The horses may not make it. They sure as hell won't make it pulling loaded wagons. Everybody will walk behind the wagons and push. You'll tie ropes to one another so if someone falls, the others will feel it. You probably won't be able to see past your noses. Yuma and I will see that the horses keep going. You just keep pushing your wagons. Every time it gets too much for you, every time you want to sink down and quit, keep remembering that making it is your one chance to stay alive when tomorrow comes."

The wind gusted sharply and flung a burst of rain over the wagons. "You've a half-hour to get yourselves ready," Fargo said, and turned away to take his weather gear from his saddlebag. He carried it with him as he stepped into Vera's wagon. She fell against him at once, and he let her cling there until he finally pushed her back. She had her rain gear laid out, and he motioned to it. "Time to get it on," he said.

"I won't be thinking about the Mescalero to keep going," Vera said. "I'll think about another night with you if we make it."

"It's a date," he told her as he donned his own gear. The rear flap of the canvas opened and he saw the four youngsters there, tied by loose lengths of rope around one another's waist.

"We're going to stay with you, Vera," the oldest boy said, but Fargo saw that she was not listening as she crossed the wagon to press her lips to his.

"So you won't forget," she murmured, and he swung out of the wagon with the sweet taste of her still with him. The wind had begun to drive harder, sending gusts of rain in at an angle that slipped beneath the branches of the hackberrys. With Yuma helping, Fargo tied the reins of each horse to the tailgate of the wagon in front of it and took the reins of the

115

lead horse into his left hand as he swung onto the pinto.

"I'll ride lead. You ride herd on the others," he told Yuma as a roar of wind all but carried his words away. The storm seemed to attack with sudden anger, as though infuriated by those who would dare its fury. Fargo moved the Ovaro back onto the passage upward, pulled gently on the reins in his left hand, and felt the horse follow. A flash of blue-white light illuminated the mountains for a split second, and the world seemed to shake with a tremendous thunder-clap. The rain became heavy, grew still heavier in what seemed but moments, and turned into a slash-ing, howling curtain of water. The night and the storm turned the world into a void of utter blackness inter-rupted only by the occasional flashes of blue-white light.

Fargo moved the Ovaro forward and kept the reins in his left hand taut so he could feel any sudden move-ment of the horse or the wagon. He rode with his head bent, but the rain had become stinging barbs that drove into his face and the ear-shattering thunder-claps seemed to shake the mountains. He moved for-ward and the storm continued to grow in intensity, increasing its fury with every flash of lightning. The gurgling sound of water as it streamed down the passage mingled with the sharper splash of the rain that cascaded like a continuous waterfall from the high rocks. The wind screamed as it whirled through the rocks, and the ground grew soft quickly.

Fargo felt the Ovaro's gait change as the horse had to lift his legs higher to pull free of the softening soil, which was quickly becoming mud. He felt the tug on the reins as the horse behind him fought for footing. He slowed, let the reins loosen, and allowed the horse to find his own pace in the shifting soil.

He seized the chance to glance back at the other

wagons as a brilliant flash of lightning turned the storm-swept night into day for a split second. One wagon rode behind the other, Yuma helping out alongside the second, and as he turned forward, the wind swept down in a vicious gust that made him seize the saddle horn to keep from sliding from the horse. The Ovaro pulled forward, and Fargo bent low in the saddle, feeling the power still in the horse's muscled legs. Water rushed down the passage now in such force that it sent up little sprays as it smashed against the Ovaro's legs. Another flash of lightning let Fargo glance up at the torrents of water that spilled down from the high rocks on both sides. If the rocks gave way, there'd be no warning, no chance to take cover, he thought. He cursed into the wind and hunched himself forward in the saddle as he tugged at the reins in his left hand.

The Ovaro moved steadily forward, continuing the slow, steady climb as it shuddered and fought against each swirling gust of wind. They'd been battling through the storm for only an hour or so, it seemed, perhaps two, but it felt as though it had been days. The world seemed to have vanished. Time, space, form, everything swallowed up in the blackness and the howl of the storm. There was only the relentless, driving rain; it slammed into his face even though he tried to keep his head down. Even the flashes of lightning had ceased, and only the world-turned-water remained. He realized he'd lost all sense of time and he measured progress only by the feel of the horse under him.

Fargo continued to lead the way up. The tautness of the reins in his left hand told him the others were still following, and he grunted in satisfaction. He had no idea of how much farther they'd gone in the timeless, inky void when he felt the Ovaro tiring. Instantly, Fargo slid from the saddle as he kept a firm grip on the

117

reins in his left hand. His feet hit the mud and he fought to keep his balance. He could see the Ovaro in front of him as the horse moved forward without the burden of a rider. Fargo glanced behind him, but the blackness and the driving rain were an impenetrable curtain. He turned back and moved after the Ovaro, the horse only a dark bulk now. He tried to hurry steps, but he slipped and went down on one knee, feeling the mud pull at him as he pushed himself to his feet. He shifted position and used the Ovaro's bulk as a shield against the wind-driven rain.

Once more he pulled himself forward, realizing only that he was completely unaware of what progress they were making. But as painfully slow as each few yards were, they were not standing still. They were still moving, and he felt a surge of pride in those behind him. He had stopped listening for the sound of rocks sliding. The wind and the sound of the rain drowned out everything else, and he pushed on, pausing as he felt the reins in his hand tighten and then return to normal tautness. He breathed a sigh of relief, pulled himself forward again, and cursed the incessant fury of the storm.

The pain in his legs came first, then the cramping of calves, and each step turned into a contest of endurance. As he grimaced with the pain, he knew those behind him couldn't go on much longer. The passage seemed to level off, but he couldn't be certain. He couldn't be certain of anything anymore, except the buffeting, debilitating power of the rain. A vicious gust of wind whipped down from a space between the crags to tear at him from the side, and he felt himself go down as his feet slipped from under him. He slid and struggled in the wet mud and only his hold on the reins prevented him from sliding backward. He used the tautness of the reins as leverage, pulled himself up on one knee and then the other, to push forward again. He lifted his head and let the rain wash the mud from his face. The others were managing to continue because, as they pushed against the rear of the wagons, they also clung and were pulled forward when they slipped.

Driving his heels deep into the mud, Fargo pushed on carefully, aware that another slip could send him sliding back under horse's hooves or wagon wheels. The Ovaro was still a dark bulk barely visible ahead of him, and Fargo felt his lips pull back in a grimace of pain and exhaustion as he fought on. Suddenly, almost with shock, he realized that the rain no longer smashed itself into his face. He raised his head and felt the rain coming down in a straight downpour, the wind ceasing. As he frowned into the dark, the rain lessened abruptly and became a veil instead of an impenetrable curtain.

He craned his neck to look back and saw the wagons still there, hardly moving now, but still there. He turned forward, relief and excitement sending a surge of new strength through him. The deep black shapes of the rocks to his right parted, and he saw an opening, an alcove between two walls of stone. He pulled at the reins in his hand, turned the horse slowly to the right, and headed for the opening. His voice lifted in a hoarse sound, but the Ovaro heard his cry, turned, and came alongside him as he led the way into the opening between the stones. The alcove was barely large enough to hold the three wagons as they crowded in, but it was level, a high-walled refuge from the water that still cascaded down the passage.

Fargo fell to his knees as the wagons halted, and he felt aching leg muscles cry out in protest. He saw Jeb White fall to the stone floor of the alcove, turn on his back, and lie in utter exhaustion as others slumped down against the wagon wheels. As the rain continued to lessen, Fargo watched the others slowly struggle to

119

their feet and begin to untie the ropes that bound each group together. The rain had all but ended, and he finally found the lone figure off to the side, head resting on knees drawn up high. Yuma looked up as he approached, and Fargo saw the utter exhaustion on the weathered face. "Sorry, old-timer," Fargo said.

"I don't plan ever to walk again," Yuma said.

"How far do you think we've come?" Fargo asked.

"Ask me something I can answer," Yuma muttered.

Fargo's eyes went skyward to where the clouds scudded along the tops of the distant peaks, and he felt the weariness weighing hard on him. He walked the half-dozen feet to Vera's wagon, winced as he climbed over the tailboard. She lay on the blanket, rain gear flung aside, and he sank down beside her. She turned to him wordlessly, buried her face against his chest, and exhaustion became a blanket that embraced them both.

He slept till he felt the warmth of the new sun through the canvas, and Vera stayed asleep as he rose and dressed and went outside. The brightness of the sun made him blink and he saw that the flaming orb had already begun to dry the ground. He walked from the stone alcove to the passage outside the rock walls and peered upward. They had come a good distance. They were in the high country, trees mostly wind-twisted scrub, the crags bordering the passage no longer towering, the higher mountain peaks no longer so distant. But the crest was still out of sight, and he swore aloud as Yuma came up, stiff-legged, to stand beside him.

"Another few hours," Yuma said. "We've bought the time. Let's use it."

"Get them up and rolling," Fargo said. He turned and went to Vera's wagon and shook her till she came awake. "Get your little butt on the driver's seat. Time to move on," he said.

"Oh, no. I can't lift my arms," she protested.

"You'll lift them. So will all of us," he said, and swung from the wagon as the others emerged, faces drawn with fatigue. He swept them with his eyes cold as the blue of a winter lake. "The Mescalero will waste some time looking for us, but as soon as they realize what happened; they'll come chasing," he told them. "The ground's still soft. They won't be able to move at top speed. I figure four hours; by midday, they'll be at the crest. That gives us two hours to get there ahead of them. Let's do it."

He turned, swung onto the Ovaro, and cantered out of the stone alcove, the warm sun a welcome blanket on flesh and bones that remained water-soaked.

Yuma came up beside him as the wagons slowly rolled from the little alcove and back on the passage. The storm had left too much loose rock and he saw the wagons jounce as they rolled over the stones that littered the upward pathway.

"We'll take it slow," Fargo said to Yuma.

"Even so, I don't think they'll have enough energy left for much fighting," Yuma said. "And to fight off the Mescalero is going to take a lot of fighting."

"Maybe not," Fargo remarked, and drew a narrowed glance from the weathered face.

"You're planning on something more than just making a stand," Yuma said. "Out with it."

"You know me too well." Fargo grinned. "I'm planning on the Mescalero doing what they don't often do; make mistakes. They're going to be riding all out for about four hours to catch us. First, they're going to be tired. Second, they're going to be steaming, raging mad."

Yuma nodded as he picked up on the rest. "The kind of mad that makes a man forget to be careful," he supplied.

"Exactly," Fargo said. "When they catch sight of

the wagons, they're going to have nothing in their minds but the rage to kill."

"You're getting as cagey as a damn cougar," Yuma grunted.

"Just hope I've figured right," Fargo said as his gaze swept the road ahead. The passage curved left, almost a full turn, and when he emerged at the other end of the curve, he uttered a sharp oath of excitement. The crest of the pass lay ahead, and he spurred the Ovaro into a trot, reaching the top as the wagons rolled into view. His eyes scanned the row of rocks that rose along the right edge of the pass where it began to curve over the crest and start down the other side. There were enough spaces between the rocks for shooting, but they were barely high enough for cover. He spit in disgust but knew he'd have to make the best of them, and he moved down to meet the wagons as they neared the crest.

He waved them to a halt as he dismounted. "Leave the wagons here," he called. "Everybody bring a rifle and follow me." He strode the half-dozen yards back to the low line of rocks at the crest and waited for the others to arrive. They halted before him, each carrying a rifle, and Fargo's eyes swept their tired, gaunt faces. He uttered a silent prayer his plan would work. The exhausted men and women before him were in no shape to fight a pitched battle with the Mescalero.

"I'm going to hitch the wagons together with one driver on the lead wagon. The rest of you will be behind those rocks," Fargo said. "When the Mescalero come charging after the wagons, you'll ambush them. If you shoot straight, you ought to take out three-quarters of them with your first volley. You either win quick or lose."

Jeb White nodded for everyone. "What about the youngsters?" he asked.

"Keep them behind the rocks with you," Fargo

said. "Stay down flat until you hear my shot. Then come up firing. But until you hear my shot, no matter what else you hear, stay down behind those rocks. Don't look up, don't try to see, don't do anything but stay flat till you hear my shot. Now get into place. You'll have about an hour more to rest."

He turned away and slid down at the edge of the line of rocks, held Vera's long glance for a moment as she passed with the others. He watched as they settled down behind the line of rocks, lying flat, positioning themselves so they could fire when the time came. He rested his head back against a tall stone and closed his eyes, let himself doze in the heat of the sun.

The air grew still, the crest a quiet, peaceful place. He rested until it was time for him to pull his eyes open, and he saw the sun high in the noon sky. He pushed himself to his feet and saw the others behind the rocks come awake at the sound. "Pick somebody to drive the wagons," Fargo said.

Jeb White rose, started to turn to the others when Vera got to her feet quickly. "I'll drive," she said simply. Jeb frowned, started to protest, but she cut him off before he uttered a word. "All the rest of you have families, kids. I've nobody but myself," she said. "I'll drive."

Jeb White's frown stayed and he glanced at the others.

"Person volunteers, they mean to do their best," Fargo interrupted. "Let's go, honey," he said to Vera, and she came to his side, walking with him as he headed down to where the wagons waited. He took her arm and she pressed close to him. "You're a good girl, Vera," he said.

She half-shrugged with a touch of embarrassment. "I'm not a very good shot, anyway," she said.

"So you think you'd make a better target?" he remarked.

Vera winced. "No, I wasn't exactly thinking that," she said.

"I'm not figuring on letting that happen, either," he said as he halted beside the last wagon. "I'll be inside, watching out the back," he said as he tethered the Ovaro to the side of the wagon. "When I call to you, drive, as fast and hard as you can," he said.

"You can bet I will," Vera said. She clung to him for a moment, pressed her lips to his, and then walked quickly back to the lead wagon.

Fargo took the big Sharps from the saddle holster as he clambered into the last wagon. Inside, he lay down and poked the barrel of the rifle through the canvas flap of the tail section as he peered out through the tiny opening. He had a clear view of the still-empty passage and he lay still, his eyes focused on where the road dropped from view. He estimated he hadn't waited more than fifteen minutes when he heard them, the soft thud of their unshod ponies an unmistakable sound. As he peered down the pass, they came into sight, racing at a full gallop. They rose as the passage rose, came into full view, riding bunched together, but he guessed there were at least fifteen.

He got to his feet, hurried through the wagon to the front seat, and pushed his head through the opening in the canvas. "Roll them, honey," he shouted, then ducked back into the wagon. He had flattened himself at the back again when he felt the sharp pull as the wagon began to roll forward. He raised the big Sharps again.

The Apache were coming fast, riding full out. His smile was made of malicious satisfaction. They were racing after the wagons exactly as he'd guessed they would, and he felt the wagon crest the top of the passage and start to roll downward. The line of rocks came into his view at his left and he smiled again. The Mescalero didn't even flick a glance at them, their murderous attention directed at the wagons which seemed to be trying to get away.

Fargo held his fire, measuring distances, as the Mescalero reached the line of rocks. His finger twitched on the trigger of the big Sharps another half-second as he let the Mescalero come fully abreast of the rocks. The Apache with the twisted mouth was half behind two others, and he chose another brow-banded target. His finger tightened on the trigger; the heavy rifle fired and he saw the Indian seem to leap backward off his racing pony. Almost instantly, the pass exploded with gunfire as the thunderous volley hurled from behind the rocks.

Fargo saw more than half the Mescalero topple from their ponies, almost as if they'd all been caught by an invisible giant lariat. He saw the others rein up in surprise, try to turn, as another fusillade of shots took down four more.

He glimpsed a rider racing past the wagon at his right and had time to see the pulled-down mouth. "Son of a bitch," Fargo shouted as he flung himself out of the rear of the wagon, held on to the tailgate with one hand, and swung himself up onto the Ovaro, which trotted alongside. He leaned forward, pulled the reins free, kicked the horse into an instant gallop, and reached the lead wagon just as the Apache fired an arrow from the other side. Fargo saw Vera dive sideways on the seat in an effort to flatten herself, and he watched the arrow tear across the top of her left shoulder. Fargo raised the big Sharps, but the Mescalero saw him and flung himself from his pony as Fargo's shot went over his head. Fargo leaned from the saddle, took the reins from Vera's hands, pulled hard, and brought the wagons to a halt. A few shots from behind told him that the few Apache left alive were racing away, and Vera started to pull herself up when the arrow smashed into the wood frame of the wagon

125

inches from her head. Fargo saw the thin line of blood from the earlier arrow that ran across her shoulder, but it was mostly a flesh wound and he leaned forward again, pushing her into the wagon. "Stay in there," he barked as he dropped from the Ovaro, the rifle in his hand, as he darted behind a rock.

His eyes swept the terrain on the other side of the crest where the Mescalero had fled. But the snarling Indian wouldn't run. He had to extract some measure of victory from his defeat. Fury and his warrior's code demanded that. Fargo darted forward again to dive behind another rock as an arrow splintered against the stone. The Indian had positioned himself behind a trio of tall rocks.

Fargo turned, stayed in a crouch as he ran to the side, and this time the arrow grazed his hat. He halted behind another stone, then ran out again. But he ran from the Mescalero, not toward him, dropped behind a log, and heard the clatter of loose rocks as the Indian moved after him. Fargo rolled into the clear for an instant, but his eyes stayed on the rocks above and he saw the Mescalero leap into view, come down on one knee, and fire another arrow from his short bow. Fargo rolled behind another rock and gave a guttural cry, pushed himself around the other edge of the rock, and saw the Mescalero half-rise, peer down, a drawn arrow on his bow.

The Indian dropped back out of sight at once, and Fargo brought the rifle up, waited in silence, his eye trained along the rifle barrel at the rock. Carefully, he shifted the rifle a fraction of an inch to the other side of the rock. He was aimed and ready as the Mescalero darted out. His shot caught the Indian in the ribs and passed through his body, and Fargo saw the Apache drop to both knees, the bow fall from his hands. He pitched onto his face, rolled over onto his back, twitched, and lay still as his gray-white tunic began to turn red. Fargo rose, stared at the Apache for another moment. The pulled-down mouth hung half-open in a final snarl.

Fargo turned and climbed across the rocky terrain to the wagons. The others had come to help Vera out, and one of the women applied a salve to the flesh wound on her shoulder as he strode up. "You did well," he said. "I'll find a spot to camp and you can sleep into the night in peace, for a change." He climbed onto the Ovaro, found a place with black oak a half-mile down the other side of the crest, and the wagons rolled into a loose triangle. He watched the others as they paused outside their wagons, and Jeb White came to him.

"We'll never forget you and Yuma for this," the man said. "I don't suppose you'll be going on with us."

"Got unfinished business back on the other side of the pass," he said. "You'll be safe from here down. The few that got away will be hightailing it back to the main camp in the foothills."

"When will you be leaving?" Zach Diamond asked.

Fargo saw Vera's little smile as he answered, "In the night sometime. Good luck to you."

"And you," the chorus answered, and he turned away, unsaddled the Ovaro, and let the dusk slide over the mountains as he stretched out on his bedroll. Exhaustion and respite brought deep sleep to the wagons, and he heard Yuma half-snore to one side of him.

The darkness began to cloak the campsite when he climbed into Vera's wagon. She woke at once and pulled down the thin sheet, her rounded little body filling his gaze with naked welcome. He sank down beside her as she sat up and took his hands, pressed them to the high, full breasts.

"That shoulder going to hurt you?" he asked.

"Not so's I'll notice," she said. She began to pull at

his clothes and in moments he was undressed beside her.

She'd been right about the shoulder, he decided later when the night was deep and he rested beside her still-panting, satiated body. She finally slept with him until he woke, rested, and she clung for a moment longer, words unneeded.

She lay with her eyes closed while he finished dressing, unwilling to watch him leave, and he smiled at her warm, firm loveliness. She'd find her own happiness, he reflected, in her own way. He swung down from the wagon, crossed to where Yuma lay. He shook the bony shoulder gently and Yuma's eyes came open.

"Time to ride, old-timer," he said. "We've a good midnight moon."

6

They rode the night through and Fargo found a shady place beneath two Douglas firs as the first pink stripes of dawn began to slide across the sky. He slept soundly and woke with the noon sun, shaking Yuma into wakefulness as he let the horses graze on a patch of mountain grass. He washed in a small stream of water that trickled over the rocks, and breakfasted on dry jerky as they took to the saddle again. "I've done my part," Yuma grumbled. "I don't know why I just don't tip my hat and go on home."

"You're curious, same as I am." Fargo laughed. "You want to know why that crew is so anxious to find Dale Talbot."

"I'll admit to that, but not curious enough to go chasing any more Mescalero. We got away in one piece so far. I don't believe in pushing my luck," Yuma said.

"Maybe we won't have to. Maybe they'll call it off when we get back," Fargo said.

"You know better'n that," Yuma snorted, and Fargo did. He headed the Ovaro down the mountains and they had reached the foothills near the day's end when he sighted the buzzards, their slow-wheeling circles unlike that of any other bird. The distaste in Yuma's face echoed his own as he moved the pinto toward the spot where the birds circled. As he drew closer, the short, square tails of the circling birds told him they were black vultures.

The path led down onto a flat stone area. Fargo reined up and felt the nausea curl in the pit of his stomach. He stared in silence at the remains of the two men, their blue uniforms in a neat pile beside each one. They had been hung by the ankles from poles, legs spread apart, their naked bodies mutilated, testicles cut off, abdomens cut from crotch to waist and entrails pulled out. The dried blood clinging to their bodies showed that the mutilation had occurred while they were still alive. The vultures had done the least harm. They had only picked at what was left.

"Goddamn Mescaleros," Yuma bit out. "They've got to make killing a damn ritual celebration."

Fargo steered around the two grisly objects that had once been two of Capt. Ellwood's troopers. "Let's do the right thing," he sighed as he swung from his horse. "Cut them down. I'll gather rocks."

Yuma obeyed without comment as Fargo amassed enough small rocks to make a single mound. He finished the task with Yuma, and it was dark as they rode on. Once again, Fargo used the moonlight to make his way down into the foothills and rested when the dawn came near. They had made good time, Fargo saw as the gray-pink light outlined the foothills. He allowed only two hours of rest and rode on with extra caution, staying away from open spaces as he circled to the bottom of the hills. He found the captain's camp exactly where he'd left it. While the place was the same, the camp had changed, he saw as four troopers on sentry duty faced him with rifles raised.

They lowered their guns as they recognized him, and he rode into a camp just waking. He tethered the Ovaro to one side and Yuma followed. The captain had put up a small field tent near where his troopers bedded down, Fargo saw, and as he slid to the ground to rest on both elbows, he saw Blossom struggle up from her bedroll, her thick blond hair shimmering in the new sun. She pulled a cotton robe around herself, took a bag and her canteen, and disappeared behind the rocks nearby, rubbing sleep from her eyes as she walked.

He was still watching the spot when she reappeared looking fresh, her face shining as she buttoned the top buttons of a light-green shirt. He saw her stop in her tracks as she spotted the Ovaro to one side of the camp. She half-spun, swept the camp with her eyes, found him, and ran toward him. She fell to the ground beside him and threw her arms around him.

"Oh, God, Fargo, am I glad to see you," she breathed, and the relief in her voice was real. She pulled back and her eyes searched his face. He had forgotten how very blue they were. "You all right?" Blossom asked.

"Fine," he said.

She leaned back on her thighs. "You get them through?" she asked, and he nodded.

"Good," Blossom said, "good." And there was satisfaction in her voice. He sensed his answer seemed a welcome omen to her. Impulsively, she threw her arms around him again, and he felt the long breasts press into him. He glanced past her and saw the others stirring, the troopers rising behind the captain's field tent.

"What's happened here? Fill me in," he said.

"God, it's been awful," Blossom said. "The captain started by taking everybody out to find the Mescalero, all of us and the whole troop."

"He find any?" Fargo questioned.

"Lots of them. Every day we'd see them, and he'd give chase and they'd disappear. It became plain they were playing games with us, letting us exhaust ourselves by chasing them up and down the hills. It was like chasing a damn pack of ghosts," Blossom said. "When the captain saw how his men were being exhausted and he wasn't getting anywhere, he decided to send out small, two-man patrols to track the Mescalero. The first patrol never came back."

"We found what was left of them," Fargo said grimly.

"Oh, God," Blossom moaned. "When they didn't come back, Ellwood decided no more patrols. He decided to stay here and wait. Then they began to raid us, just quick, passing attacks. They'd appear, fire, and disappear, sometimes on foot, sometimes on horseback. Sometimes he'd take the troop after them. He lost two more troopers that way. He set up twenty-four-hour sentry rings then and holed up here. It's been terrible, really terrible."

"Why didn't he pull out?" Fargo asked.

"First, the senator insisted we stay," Blossom said, and she made a wry face. "Then I told him what I thought."

"What was that?"

"I told him that he was piss-scared, that none of that army-manual shit has worked worth a damn here, and that he was in way over his head," Blossom snapped angrily.

"Say anything else to comfort him?" Fargo remarked.

"Sure. I told him to pray you get the hell back here," she said, and Fargo laughed, pushed himself to his feet, and pulled her up with him.

"And you still want to try to find Dale Talbot?" he asked.

"Yes. The others all still want to find him, too. But I want you to find him first. For me," Blossom said. "That's why I hired you, and that still goes."

Fargo glanced past her and saw a figure step from the small field tent. He realized that it was the captain, but his face grown ten years older in what seemed overnight. Drawn lines had been etched onto the captain's smooth cheeks, his lips were pressed down tight, and his shoulders bent forward, but the age was mostly in the eyes, which stared at the big man almost as though he were a ghost.

"When did you get back?" the captain asked.

"Few hours ago," Fargo said.

The captain halted in front of him. Blossom had been right: there was fear in the officer's eyes. Fargo's glance flicked past Capt. Ellwood at the senator's portly figure as he emerged from the field tent. The man's frown was instant as he marched forward.

"Heard you've been having trouble," Fargo said.

"Dammit, Fargo, this is all your fault," Sen. Talbot roared. "You're supposed to be the expert. You should've been here helping us. That's what you were paid for."

Fargo smiled pleasantly. "Senator, go screw yourself," he said.

The senator's face grew florid, and he sputtered, finally swallowed words, and glared at the big man. "You're back. You going to help us?" he snapped.

"Depends," Fargo answered.

"They know we're here. They're watching us. How can we find their camp now?" Capt. Ellwood asked.

"Takes doing it the right way. They're not watching you every minute, night and day," Fargo said.

"If you can find their camp, locate it for me, I could charge them with the whole troop. We could at least rescue Dale Talbot, if he's there," the captain said, excitement catching at his voice.

"I don't know about charging their camp, but finding it comes first. I'll try," he said, and saw Blossom watching him carefully.

"What can I do? Send some troopers with you?" the captain asked earnestly.

"Hell, no," Fargo answered in alarm. "You just stay here and keep your sentry details on."

"I will, though they haven't bothered us lately," the captain said.

"They've no need to," Fargo said. "They know you've got to make some move sooner or later. They can afford to wait." His eyes went past the captain and saw Downs and Robertson listening, standing together. They continued to remain the most disciplined of the lot, clothes still neat, expressions showing neither alarm nor elation, a certain calm appraisal radiating from both men. Fargo's eyes went to Olive, who had come up to listen. Lines of tension pulled at her face and her heavy breasts seemed to sag against the dark-brown shirt she wore, and she suddenly looked every bit her age.

"Sorry you came?" he asked as he stepped closer to her.

"It was the thing to do," Olive remarked, the reply an indirect answer that said nothing more.

Fargo turned from her and went to the Ovaro, beckoned to Blossom as he adjusted the saddle skirt. "You're out of time," he said to Blossom when she reached him.

"For what?" Blossom frowned.

"For phony stories, for quick lies. I want to know the real reason why you're all trying to find Dale Talbot. I want the truth about you and whatever you know about the others. No more holding back on anything," Fargo growled.

She looked at the hardness in his eyes with her own frowning truculence. "All right," she said finally. "You find the camp and I'll tell you everything you want to know. I'll tell you why I want to get to him first, and everything else. But I want to be sure you found their camp first. Fair enough?"

"All right, fair enough," he grunted. "You just be

ready to talk when I get back." She nodded happily, squeezed his arm as he swung onto the Ovaro. He waved to Yuma, who sat watching from beneath a small shrub, and rode from the campsite, turned the Ovaro south along the edge of the foothills. He kept moving south till he guessed he'd gone far enough, then turned the pinto up in the long, narrow passages between the rocks. He moved up and slowly worked his way back northward, threaded his way from one crevice to another.

He paused often, stayed hidden, listened, sniffed the air, and then continued to edge his way up the foothills. Finally, he slid from the Ovaro, keeping the horse out of sight in the narrow depths of the passageway as he pulled himself up to a flat rock sheltered by a small ledge. The spot gave him an unbroken view of the dips and rises of the foothills, and he settled onto his stomach. He felt the heat of the sun burning into his back at once and he lay still and silent as a chuckwalla. But his eyes ceaselessly swept the foothills, picking out the bare-chested horsemen that moved singly or in pairs across the rocky terrain. He watched as they came into sight, and he stayed with each and noted their paths as he drew a line on a chart inside his mind.

As the day finally drew to a close, his lips pulled into a smile. There was a pattern. They wandered, crossing over one another's paths, but they returned in a pattern, their trails moving down to one spot. Fargo let the night descend before he slid down to where he'd left the Ovaro. When he did, he steered the horse through the maze of passages in the rocks until he neared the spot he had marked in his mind.

An almost full moon came up, and he moved the horse downward and grunted silently in satisfaction. The path's end merely confirmed what he had put together as he'd watched. Twin hills rose opposite each other, identical in height and shape, and between them, nestled in the hollow and surrounded by rock formations, was the Apache camp.

He actually smelled it before it came into sight, the odor of mesquite burning, the slightly acrid smell of lizard meat being cooked. He slid from the saddle, put the Ovaro into a rock fissure, and crept closer on foot. The camp sprawled in the rocky hollow, no line camp but a major base with three wickiups and a small tent, a rack for drying meat in the sun. He saw a half-dozen squaws putting out two small fires and the men beginning to lay down on the ground while a few drifted into the wickiups. A half-dozen gambel oaks dotted the perimeter of the camp, and Fargo saw the squaws file into another of the wickiups. His glance went to two men who began to climb up the rocks until they reached a ledge that extended over the camp. They settled down there, eyes focused on the broad passageway to the south, which led directly to the camp. From where they were positioned, they could scan the approach to the camp from any direction, but they couldn't see down into the camp itself. He made a mental note of this fact as his eyes swept the camp again. He saw no sign of Dale Talbot, but the man could be held inside one of the wickiups or the lone tent, he realized.

Fargo took a final survey of the camp and made his way back down to the fissure where he'd left the Ovaro. He led the Ovaro until it was safe enough to ride, and he half-circled away from the Apache camp until he'd reached the base of the foothills. As he looked back, the twin hills side by side were now a clear marker, and he spurred the horse into a canter. He held the pace until he rode into sight of Capt. Ellwood's campsite and reined to a halt as four sentries rose with rifles leveled. They recognized him as he neared, lowered their guns, and let him come

136

through. He pulled over to one side of the camp, saw that most everyone was asleep, but the blond hair came out of the bedroll as he began to unsaddle the Ovaro. Yuma, he saw, slept soundly a dozen yards away, and he heard Blossom's barefoot steps as she hurried up to him. She halted and her eyes searched his face.

"You've some talking to do," he said to her as he put the saddle on the ground.

"You found the camp," she gasped with excitement, and her arms were around his neck at once.

"Didn't see any sign of Dale Talbot," he told her. "But he could've been inside one of the wickiups."

Blossom hugged him to her and he felt the warmth of her breasts pushing into his shirt. "Where is it?" she asked. "Very far from here?"

"About an hour's ride," he said, pointing to the twin peaks that rose up in perfect balance under the moon. "Right smack between those two hills there. I'm listening," he said severely, pulling her arms down from around his neck.

Blossom turned to look back at the camp and Fargo saw Downs and Robertson sitting up on their bedrolls. She turned back to him, her eyes round. "It'll take a good deal of telling and I don't want them to see us talking. Besides, the others just turned in. Wait till they're all asleep—say at midnight," Blossom said. "You can grab some shut-eye till then. You've got to be tired."

He nodded, the thought appealing at once as he welcomed the idea of a few hours' sleep. "Midnight," he grunted. "You be here."

"Promise," Blossom said, kissed him quickly, and hurried back to her bedroll. It was perhaps just as well others didn't see her telling everything to him, he reasoned as he lay down flat on the ground, stretched his body, and felt the weariness in it. He slept quickly and soundly, dimly aware only of the sentries exchanging a few words from time to time. But he had set the inner timing mechanism he had learned to master long ago, and the moon was in the midnight sky when he snapped awake and sat up.

He strained his eyes, peered across the camp, and saw the shape still under Blossom's blanket. Damn girl was still asleep, he grunted. Or was hoping he'd stay asleep. Damned if she was going to weasel out of the bargain, he grumbled as he rose and walked to her blanket. He halted beside it and felt the frown dig into his brow. Not even a stray strand of thick blond hair escaped from the top of the blanket. Even as he looked up to see the big gray, he knew what he'd find: the horse was gone. He swore aloud as he yanked the blanket down and stared at the little pile of clothes under it. He swore more loudly as Yuma came up. "Now, that is one stupid, stubborn, hard-nosed idiot of a girl," Fargo said. "She's gone off to trade her trinkets for Dale Talbot."

"No shit," Yuma said.

"That was her idea from the start, but I didn't figure she was still thinking about doing it," Fargo said. "Goddamn her stupid hide. Now I've got to go save her neck, if I still can."

"Why? She's her own damn fool. No need for you to be one, too," Yuma answered.

"That's just it, she's being a damn fool, but she's not like the others. She was the only one who rode out to wish us well taking the wagons through. Her heart's in the right place. It's only her head that's screwed on backward. That makes her worth a try at saving," Fargo said.

"Maybe," Yuma grunted. "What are you figuring that'll involve my hide?"

"If I'm too late, I'll be back before morning. If I'm not back, wake up Ellwood. He's ready to listen to you. The Mescalero camp is right between those two hills. They've sentries watching the one wide approach. You have Ellwood mount a full charge right up that path at the camp," Fargo said.

"Their sentries will alert them and they'll come out in full at us," Yuma said. "Ellwood doesn't have enough troopers."

"I know that. Soon as you see the Mescalero, you turn and hightail it back here. They'll stop when they see you running. They won't go chasing into anything that might be a dry gulch," Fargo said.

"All you want is their attention on us so you can get Blossom," Yuma said.

"Bull's-eye," Fargo said as he walked to the Ovaro and began to saddle the horse.

"What if Ellwood won't go for it?" Yuma asked.

"Tell him I'll feed him to the Mescalero or shoot him myself," Fargo growled.

"My pleasure," Yuma said as Fargo swung onto the horse.

Fargo laughed as he started the Ovaro out of the camp. He paused at the four sentries. "Why the hell did you let the girl leave camp?" He frowned.

"She said she was going on your orders," one of the troopers answered. "Besides, we've no orders from the captain to stop anybody from leaving."

"Guess not," Fargo grunted as he sent the Ovaro into a trot, then changed to a fast canter as he headed for the twin hills in the distance. He rode more openly under cover of the night until he neared the hills and turned the horse into the cracks and fissures of the rocks terrain. He circled, stayed away from the wide approach to the hollow, made his way around to the side of the camp, and threaded through rocky fractures until he dismounted and led the Ovaro to the fissure near the camp. He left the horse out of sight and moved forward on foot, finding a rock tall enough to let him take cover at the edge of the camp. Only one thing had changed from his last visit just a few hours ago—a naked blond-haired figure was now tied to a pole near one of the wickiups.

Nearly naked, Fargo corrected himself. For some reason, they had left Blossom's white bloomers on her. But she was alive, he breathed in relief, a few bruises on her long breasts. They were saving her for the full treatment, probably at sundown tomorrow, he thought, then grimaced. Rawhide thongs bound her ankles and wrists to the pole so that she could only kneel or sit back on her legs. He saw the extra pack she had brought tossed aside with a few of the baubles still clinging to it, and he let his glance scan the camp again. Horses, along with Blossom's big gray, were tethered just in back of the nearby wickiup and a dozen Mescalero lay asleep on the ground at the other side of the camp, another group at the front part of the hollow.

He brought his eyes back to the opposite side of the camp as two more Apache appeared, each with a lance in hand. They walked as a pair, and as he watched, they moved silently on, along the outer edge of one of the wickiups, down past the small, lone tent, past more sleeping figures. They were patrolling the outside perimeter of the camp, he realized, and moved back from the rock and into a crevice.

He watched them come into view again, walk past Blossom, and he heard one utter a derisive snort. They disappeared into the darkness at the other end of the hollow. Fargo stayed in the crevice and watched them make three circles of the entire campsite as he ticked seconds off in his mind. Each full circle took about three minutes, and as they passed him for the fourth time, he moved forward in silent steps that brought him up behind Blossom. He reached out, clapped a hand around her mouth from behind, and felt her body stiffen.

"It's me. Be quiet," he hissed, and she nodded. He withdrew his hand and crept forward to crouch beside her.

"Oh, God, Fargo," Blossom whispered.

"How'd the trading go?" he hissed as his eyes swept the opposite side of the camp. "Little one-sided, was it?" he said, glancing at her to see the half-pout come into her face. "You know, you are one dumb-assed dish," he said.

"Get me out of here," she whispered.

"No way now," he said. "If you're gone when those two come by, we won't get out of these foothills alive. You've got to stick around awhile longer."

"Till when?" Blossom asked.

"Morning," Fargo said.

"Morning?" she echoed in dismay.

"I hope," he bit out. "Work on your trading pitch."

"Fargo . . ." she gasped, a strained whisper.

"Quiet," he snapped as the two Apache came into sight across the camp. He swung himself behind Blossom, hid there as the two sentries moved on past the tent. He patted her rear with one hand. "Keep the faith, baby," he whispered, and shrunk back silently until he was closeted in the fissure with the Ovaro. He settled himself there and rested his back against the rock wall, half-closed his eyes.

Dawn seemed to take forever to arrive, but he finally saw the first gray glint peer over the high peaks. He rose, edged himself from the rock fissure until he could see the camp, crawled his way a few yards closer on his belly, and halted behind the tall rock.

The two sentries had stopped patrolling as the camp came awake under the light of the new day. Four half-naked squaws came out of one of the wickiups, one fairly young and firm-breasted, the other three wrin-

141

kled old hags with flapping appendages for breasts. The young one fetched fruit out of a reed basket and began handing it to the men who came over. Two of the old hags walked to Blossom, halted, jabbered at her. As he watched, one kicked out suddenly, her foot landing in Blossom's ribs, and Fargo heard her yelp of pain. The squaws laughed and the other hag stepped closer, drew a bone hunting knife from the waist of her skirt, and cut off a piece of Blossom's thick blond hair. She walked off holding it up triumphantly, the other following.

Fargo saw Blossom turn her head, fear and panic in her face as her eyes darted around in search of him. He grimaced and wondered where the hell the captain and his troop were as the morning began to spread over the foothills. He felt his hands pressed hard against the rock as he cursed silently. Minutes suddenly seemed hours, and he saw the panic grow in Blossom's face. He started to swear silently again when a shout interrupted, the cry one of alarm from the high rocks above. The sentries had caught sight of the column charging up the wide path, and Fargo saw the camp erupt.

The men raced for the ponies. A figure stepped from the lone tent, two eagle feathers in his brow-band, an imposing man despite the shortness of his height. He barked commands and one of the others rode up with a pony for him. He leapt onto it in one bound and led the way as the Mescalero swept from the camp and onto the wide approach at the far end.

The pathway had a slight rise and the sentries had spotted the captain's troopers when they first entered the mouth of the passage. Fargo estimated it'd be another two or three minutes before Ellwood and Yuma saw the Mescalero racing toward them, reined up, and hightailed it back. The Mescalero would give chase for perhaps another two minutes before they halted in caution. That gave him maybe six minutes, he thought. He'd need every one of them to cut Blossom free and gain some distance before the Mescalero returned and found her gone. They'd realize what had happened and be raging mad about it, he knew.

He drew the double-bladed throwing knife from its calf holster as he rose, ran forward in a crouch, and fell to one knee beside Blossom. He had the two ankle thongs cut when he heard the scream and saw the squaws staring at him. Four others came running from one of the other wickiups. Screaming and gesticulating, they started to run at him, and he saw three of them pick up sticks, two more with scraping knives in their hands, one with a bone hunting knife.

"Dammit," he swore as the last thong proved stubborn. It finally severed and Blossom rolled, got to her feet. "Get your horse," he said, and she ran.

The screaming squaws were almost on him, but he kept the Colt holstered. A shot now would certainly bring some of the Mescalero racing back. He yanked at the pole that had held Blossom, pulled it from the ground, and swung it in an arc. It caught the first three squaws as they flung themselves at him and he saw them double over and go down. Two more had skirted to one side and came at him from the right. He pulled the pole back, ducked, and kicked out at a fairly young squaw who rushed him. His boot caught her in the belly and she went down with a gasp, and it gave him time to bring the pole around and slam it into the side of the other squaw's head. She fell sideways with a scream of pain and anger.

He looked up and saw Blossom on the big gray. But the old hag with the hunting knife, lips drawn back over toothless gums, raced at him with the knife raised, two of the others close at her heels. Fargo leapt backward to give himself more room, brought the pole around, and used it as a lance. He thrust forward with it, all the strength of his powerful shoulder muscles behind the blow. It hit the old hag in the center of her scrawny abdomen, tore through flesh and brittle old tendons, and she gave a gargled scream as she fell back and crashed into the other two. She went down with them, the pole sticking up from her midsection as though she were an old hen skewered on a spit.

Fargo turned, ran and saw Blossom follow on the gray. He raced to the crevice, climbed onto the Ovaro, headed the horse out onto the flat rocks, and turned south. He galloped along a smooth passage, then slowed as he threaded down into another narrow chasm that led to a flat area.

Blossom rode at his heels, her long breasts swaying as she raced after him, blond hair flying back from her face. Another time, another place, and he would've stopped and taken her, for she managed to look improperly beautiful. But he kept the Ovaro racing where the terrain allowed it; then he slowed and made his way down through narrow chasms that took them down and south to the bottom of the foothills.

Finally, satisfied they had gone beyond the area the Mescalero would search in their first flush of frustrated anger, he pulled to a halt beneath a cluster of hackberry trees and slid to the ground. Blossom swung from the gray, her round little rear wiggling, delved into her saddlebag, and pulled out a blue shirt and a gray skirt she slipped on at once.

"Stubborn's one thing; plain stupid's another," Fargo muttered when she finished dressing.

She cast him a glance that still held stubbornness as well as contrition in it. "I always heard you could trade with the Indians. I had things with me I thought they'd be happy to trade for," she said.

"The Apache don't trade when they can take," Fargo snapped. "Why the hell should they?"

"I never thought about it that way." Blossom blinked.

"You never thought," he said. "You don't even speak the language. How the hell were you going to find out anything about Dale Talbot?"

"I had a picture of him with me, a drawing that was his," she said. "I showed it to them. He's dead. They killed him," she said, and her voice lowered. "They used sign language anybody could understand," she said, and drew her finger across her throat.

"You find out anything else?" Fargo asked, and she shook her head. "You were going to tell me things," he snapped. "Start with the senator. I've been wondering if he's really Talbot's brother."

"They're brothers, all right," Blossom said as she folded herself on the ground beside a log. "But they hated each other."

"So why is the senator so all-fired anxious to find out what happened to Dale?" Fargo questioned.

"Not Dale," Blossom said with a wry laugh. "What Dale had with him." Fargo waited, his frown questioning. "Senator Talbot's a crook. He's been using his position to work every kind of crooked government deal you can think of; kickbacks, favors, selling land with phony deeds, giving secret government information to friends of his so they could make a killing in railroad stocks. You name a shady deal, and he's been part of it. But he's been clever, awful clever. Only Dale knew his brother from way back, and he knew how the senator operated."

"So he decided to get the goods on him," Fargo said.

"That's right." Blossom nodded. "Dale set up an office in Washington and kept special track of everything the senator did. He got the facts, the names, and the figures. He got things no one else could've gotten because he knew how his brother thought, moved, operated."

"And he was going to blackmail the senator with it," Fargo said.

Blossom nodded again. "The senator got a kickback or a piece of every shady deal. He's loaded. Dale figured he'd pay well to keep on pulling off his deals. He was on his way to Mexico when the Apache caught him. Mexico is a place where the senator couldn't touch him."

"Where the hell do you fit in?" Fargo asked.

"Dale and I were sort of keeping company at the time. He promised me half of everything his brother paid him if I could get the money he needed to set up his office, pay certain people, and get the goods on the senator. My mother had some land in Kentucky. I took a mortgage out on it without telling her."

"And old Dale skipped out on you, too." Fargo almost laughed.

Blossom made a face. "Yes, the bastard," she hissed. "But I knew he was going to Mexico. I was following when I heard about the Apache attack. I decided to go on and try to find if he was still alive."

"And all the senator wants is to make sure that the evidence Dale Talbot had isn't still lying around where somebody can pick it up," Fargo said, and Blossom nodded. "One more piece; Olive Reamer, why is she with the senator?" he asked.

"The senator never kept actual figures himself. He was too cagey for that. Olive did all the record-keeping. As his secretary, she knew everything—who, where, when, and how much—and she kept the records herself. He brought Olive along because if he found Dale alive, Olive would be the only one who'd know if they were taking back the right stuff," Blossom said.

"You find out what happened to whatever Dale had

with him when the Apache killed him?" Fargo queried.

"No," Blossom said. "I know he had two briefcases, but I didn't see them at the camp and I couldn't make them understand about them."

"I'll be dammed." Fargo frowned. "I've been putting my neck on the line for a bunch of crooks; a corrupt senator and his involved secretary, an ambitious army captain, and a greedy little blond. Am I glad I took those settlers through. They were the only ones who deserved help."

"I'm not like the others," Blossom protested.

"Not so's I can see," Fargo answered.

"I came after Dale Talbot to get the money back for the mortgage I took on my mother's land. I figured he owed me that. That's all I wanted, I'd decided," Blossom said.

"You weren't thinking of carrying on his little blackmail scheme if you got the goods in your hot little hands?" Fargo tossed back.

"No," Blossom said angrily. "I wouldn't have known how to go about it. I just wanted that mortgage money he owed me, and I don't care if you believe me or not."

"Good, 'cause I'm not in a believing mood," Fargo said. "You forgot to tell me about Downs and Robertson."

"I don't know where they fit in. Honest I don't. I never knew of Dale working for any bank," she said.

"I've an idea where they fit—more so now," Fargo said. "Get your ass in the saddle. We're heading back to camp."

Blossom brought the gray up to ride alongside him as he turned north and stayed close to the rocks at the bottom of the foothills. The Mescalero had called off their search for now, he was certain. But they wouldn't forget, he knew.

Blossom rode in silence, a pout on her face. He had the feeling she was telling the truth about wanting only the mortgage money back. A complex blackmail scheme took more savvy than she had. But he wasn't certain and he wasn't about to tell her so in any case.

They were almost at the campsite when she spoke up. "I wish you'd believe me."

"Why? Wouldn't change all that much," he growled.

"It'd make a difference to me," she said softly.

"I'll think about it," he told her as they rode into sight of the camp.

The captain had every trooper up and on guard, Fargo saw, and he dismounted as Yuma hurried up to him.

"Damn, you pulled it off," Yuma chortled.

"So far," Fargo said.

"Find out what you wanted to know?" Yuma asked.

"Too much," Fargo muttered, and drew the old man off to one side. He recounted what Blossom had told him, and Yuma frowned at him when he finished.

"I'll be a sidewinder's uncle," Yuma rasped. "If that doesn't beat all. That does it for me. I'm pulling out."

"Wait a few minutes more. Might be some fireworks yet," Fargo said as he saw Capt. Ellwood emerge from the small field tent, the senator and Olive right behind him. The senator brushed past the captain in his haste to confront Blossom.

"You see Dale?" he barked.

"He's dead. They killed him," Blossom said coldly.

"Any of his things there?" Sen. Talbot questioned.

Fargo held the smile inside himself.

"Two of his shirts and his boots," Blossom said. "Nothing else."

The senator thought for a moment and his eyes were shrewd as he turned to Fargo. "I've heard that when the Apache take things they can't use or don't want, they often bring them to a trading post and sell them for something they want; whiskey, guns, steel knives," he said.

"They do that sometimes," Fargo said blandly.

"Is there such a trading post around here?" the senator asked.

"Joe Tortillos'," Fargo said, and glanced at Yuma. "Due south of here at the end of the Sacramento Mountains, right, Yuma?" he said.

Yuma stared back for a moment, and then Fargo saw the flicker in his eyes. "Right," Yuma said. "Directly south."

"Then that's where we'll go at once," the senator said to Capt. Ellwood.

Fargo saw the captain frown, but he kept his smile hidden. The senator's eagerness made sense only because of what Blossom had told him, and he watched the perplexity in the captain's once-young face.

"Why would you want to go there, Senator?" Ellwood asked.

"Dale's gone. Maybe I could still find something of his to keep in memory of him; a watch, cuff links, anything," the senator said, and let his voice grow sober.

"How about a briefcase?" Fargo offered affably.

The senator's eyes darkened for an instant, but he was smooth and quick, Fargo saw. "Any memento would do," the senator said sadly.

"Memento, my ass," Fargo snapped. "Why don't you tell the captain the truth?"

The senator's face began to grow red as Fargo fastened his eyes on Ambrose Ellwood.

"The senator's a goddamn crook," Fargo said, and repeated everything Blossom had told him. When he finished, he let his eyes rest on Sen. Talbot.

"Lies, every damn word of it," the senator roared, and Fargo found himself admiring the man's resilience. "I don't know what this woman's game is, but she's a bold, brazen liar. I think she's working for someone trying to ruin my reputation," the senator went on. "It's plain this man is her accomplice. He risked your entire troop to save her." He focused his full attention on the captain. "Step into your tent with me, Captain. What I have to say to you is confidential," he said, and marched into the tent. The captain followed obediently.

Fargo let his glance roam over the others. Downs and Robertson were quiet, contained. Olive stared at the ground and Blossom bit her lower lip nervously. Some of the nearby troopers seemed uncomfortable. Fargo relaxed, saw Yuma watching from the side, and then the captain finally step from the field tent again.

"I'm afraid I have to take the word of a United States senator over that of some strange girl," the captain said.

Fargo's eyes grew hard. "What'd he offer you in there, Ellwood?" he speared.

The captain drew himself up stiffly. "The senator pointed out to me the unreliability of unsubstantiated charges," he said.

"Bullshit. He pointed out to you that you'd gone this far and you were in up to your neck and you'd better play ball with him," Fargo rasped.

"You watch your tongue, Fargo. I don't have to take that. I can have you put in irons," Capt. Ellwood shouted.

Fargo turned away, the contempt in his face his only reply. "You all going chasing with the captain, again?" he asked the others. Olive nodded, of course, but he saw the apology in her eyes, and he smiled at her. Apology and admission, but she had to go on with the charade. "You, too?" he asked Downs and Robertson.

"We're obligated," Robertson said smoothly. "We have to see if any of the bank's papers are still there."

"Of course you do," Fargo said, and turned to Blossom.

She met his questioning gaze, and he saw her study his face for a long moment. "Sorry," she said. "I have to go along."

"You're full of surprises, aren't you, honey?" Fargo frowned. "You thinking of trying to work a deal with the senator?"

She didn't answer, turned away with her eyes averted, and Fargo laughed as he walked to where Yuma waited to mount his sturdy little quarter horse.

"I'll be going back. I've had enough," Yuma said.

"Thanks for helping," Fargo said.

"They're going to have a hard time finding Joe Tortillos at the end of the Sacramento, seeing as his place was in White Sands last time I looked," Yuma said, grinning.

"I guess so." Fargo chuckled.

Yuma's laugh was an echo as he rode away.

7

Fargo lay stretched out along the edge of the campsite as through half-closed eyes he watched Capt. Ellwood and Sen. Talbot outside the tent.

"We'll be heading due south, away from the heart of Mescalero country," the senator said. "We can get started at once."

"No, the men and the horses need at least a few hours' rest. We'll head out in late afternoon. I want the men alert in case the Mescalero try to attack. You never know," Capt. Ellwood said.

Fargo nodded in agreement as he stretched, let himself half-doze. It was midafternoon when he woke to the sound of the troopers breaking camp. He rose, his eyes scanning the foothills. Nothing moved and he felt the uneasiness pull at him. He felt the captain come up behind him, and turned.

"Frankly, Fargo, when Major Carpenter returns, I'll strongly recommend he never hire you to work for the army again," the captain said.

"That's all right. I don't plan to have much of anything good to tell him about you. Some whores wear dresses, some wear uniforms," Fargo said.

The captain's mouth almost trembled in fury as he stalked away. Fargo watched him mount up and move the troop on. The senator and the others rode alongside; Fargo's eyes followed Blossom, but she didn't look back. He made a harsh sound. She had surprised him again. Yet there was something wrong. She had been contrite, anxious that he believe her, and he'd felt the honesty of that. Then she'd snapped at the chance to maybe make a deal for herself. It had been almost too quick, too abrupt a reversal. It didn't hang together. Some women could change like chameleons, he knew, but Blossom had been the opposite, absolutely unswerving in her stubbornness. Maybe that was it, he concluded. She was simply clinging to her goal. Yet it didn't satisfy.

He watched the column ride away on the flatland bordering the foothills until it was out of sight, and he lay down on the ground again, stretched his still-tired muscles, and waited for the night to come. When it finally blanketed the land, he rose and headed the Ovaro up into the foothills. He traveled southeast, toward the end of the Sacramento Mountains, just as the column had headed, but toward the other side of the last of the foothills. He rode slowly, carefully, pausing often to listen, and a tight little smile began to edge his lips.

It was nearly midnight when he halted in a rocky hollow and set his bedroll in the deepest shadows of tall rocks at one side. He pushed clothes into the bedroll and placed his hat over the top, and keeping in the black shadows, he climbed around the edge of the tallest rock and crouched on his haunches, the big Colt in his hand. He'd been aware for the last few hours that he was being followed. Every time he had halted and listened, he'd caught the sound of another horse being reined up. Only a split-second difference, yet always enough to let him catch the sound of a hoofbeat as the horse halted. Horse or horses, he couldn't be sure which. He stayed crouched, silent and unseen, knowing he had only to wait. The figures finally came into sight—two of them, on foot—and edged their way into the hollow. They bent low as they approached his bedroll against the rocks, guns in hand.

"Fargo, come out slow. We don't want trouble," the one said.

"Then drop your guns," Fargo answered softly, and saw the two figures spin, peer into the blackness of the shadows. "Drop the guns," Fargo repeated, his voice harsher. The two figures dropped their guns, backed away, and Fargo leapt down out of the deep shadows to land lightly on the balls of his feet. "Mister Downs and Mister Robertson," he said. "Don't be mad at yourselves. You didn't do a bad job of tailing. Would've worked with most people."

"Thanks," Downs said wryly.

"I kind of thought it might be you two. How are things at the agency?" Fargo asked, and laughed as the two men exchanged glances of surprise.

"How long have you known?" Robertson asked.

"Suspected almost from the start. It's not that hard to spot a Pinkerton man if you know what to look for. Couldn't figure what brought you here, though. Still can't," Fargo said.

"The Justice Department hired us. They've had the senator under suspicion for a long time, ever since a particular beef deal. But they didn't want to use their own agents. They were afraid some of the senator's connections might spot them," Robertson told him. "When we heard he was headed out here to find his brother, we knew there had to be more reason than that, so we decided to stay on top of him."

"What made you come after me tonight?" Fargo asked.

Downs smiled. "You knew why the senator wanted the address of that trading post. You'd no reason to give it to him unless you were sending him off on a wild-goose chase. The detective mind. We are professionals, after all." Fargo laughed and nodded agreement. "We guessed you'd some move of your own planned."

"If those papers were at Joe Tortillos', I figured to get them into the hands of a U.S. marshal," Fargo said.

"May we pick up our guns, Fargo? We've no quarrel between us," Robertson said.

"No," a voice cut in sharply. "Leave the guns where they are. Throw yours out with them, Fargo," the voice ordered.

Fargo swore softly. "Goddamn," he said. "Blossom, what the hell are you doing here?" He started to turn.

"Don't move. Throw the gun out," Blossom said tersely.

Fargo blew breath from his lips as he tossed the Colt on the ground and Blossom stepped into sight, a big, old Walker in her hand. He glared at her. "What brought you following me?" he asked.

"Detectives' mind for them, woman's intuition for me," Blossom said. "You backed off too easily. It wasn't at all like you, Fargo. I knew you had to be up to something. When the captain made camp, I stayed awake and saw these two gents sneak off. They followed you and I followed them."

"Miss Daley, work with us on this thing," Robertson said.

"Why? What happens if you get those papers?" Blossom asked.

"Frankly, I don't think they exist any longer. I think the Mescalero just tossed Dale Talbot's things away. We're only going on to be absolutely certain," Robertson said.

"You didn't answer me. What happens if they exist and you get them?" Blossom insisted.

"We turn them over to the Justice Department," Downs answered.

"And I don't get my mortgage money back," Blossom said.

"I'm afraid not," Downs said. "That was a private matter between you and Dale Talbot."

"Forget it. If that stuff is there, I'm getting it. I can sell it to any newspaper or journal and get my mortgage money out of it," she said, and turned her eyes on Fargo. "I told you, that's all I want."

"Blossom, you do keep your eye on the ball, I must say," Fargo admitted.

"I'm sorry, but that's the way it has to be. I don't get that money, my ma loses her land," Blossom said. "Turn around, all of you."

"Blossom, you don't want to do this. What if the Mescalero find us?"

"We're out of Mescalero country," she said.

"Hell we are. They're going to be looking for revenge. They'll be all over," Fargo said.

"Don't try to play on my sympathies, Fargo," she said, and he saw her take a quick step forward, bring the butt of the Colt down on Robertson's head. The man toppled and she slammed the gun on Downs' head. He fell half over Robertson. Fargo watched her step back, move directly behind him.

"Blossom, you may have to live with this the rest of your life," Fargo said.

"Shut up, damn you. I've got to do what I have to do," Blossom snapped. His reply was cut off as he felt the heavy Walker crash down on his head. Purple and yellow lights flashed in his mind for a moment and he was dimly aware he was falling forward and the world spun away, the flashing lights clicked off, and there was nothingness.

He felt the tug on his arm first, and his eyes came open. "Jesus," he groaned. His head hurt and he cursed blonds in general. He focused his gaze and saw

Downs had come around as Robertson groaned, fought his way to consciousness. They were tied together, wrapped up in yards of lariat, arms pinned to their sides, legs bound, and all three of them lashed as one. Fargo saw dawn sliding across the sky and heard Downs groan. "God, we'll be all day getting loose," he said.

"Damn little bitch," Fargo swore.

"She is that," Downs said, "but you've got to admire that kind of single-minded purpose."

"I'd like to fan her single-minded little ass," Fargo growled, and tugged at the ropes with no results. The morning broke quickly, and he saw Blossom had left their guns on the ground. She expected they'd eventually work their way loose, he noted with grim apprehension.

Robertson wriggled to a sitting position and took Downs and Fargo with him. "Let's pull in different directions," he said, and Fargo nodded. He pulled his body to the right, Robertson pulled left, and Downs, in the center, pulled backward. Fargo felt himself draw a long breath when he stopped. "Feel anything loosen?" Robertson asked.

"Not a damn thing," Fargo muttered. "She's got us wrapped up like mummies." His eyes swept the hollow, came to rest on the rough side of the quartz rock formations. "Let's get over there and start rubbing the ropes against those rocks," Fargo said. "I figure we ought to get them frayed enough to break in a few hours."

"Let's go," Downs said.

Fargo leaned back, used his bound ankles to press his heels into the ground. He felt Downs try to do the same and suddenly he was half-rolled on his side.

"This isn't going to be that easy," Downs muttered. "It'll take coordination."

The man's words proved to be an understatement.

The quartz rocks only a few yards away began to seem unreachable as the three men pushed, leaned, strained to move as one, and finally mastered the way to inch themselves forward without losing their collective balance.

When they reached the rocks, Fargo heard Robertson gasp in air and Downs wheeze as his own breath came hard. He waited for everyone to gather themselves. "Now push up, backs against the rocks," he said finally, timed his push with Downs and Robertson, and felt his back come against the rough quartz. "Left and right, left and right, everybody together," he said, and began to rub against the rocks. They'd worked at it for some fifteen minutes, halted to rest, when the sound drifted up from the flatland below, distant but unmistakable.

"Rifle fire," Downs said.

Fargo listened and heard the sound grow closer, louder. "Army carbines," he grunted, the edge of bitterness in his words. The sounds died away, erupted again, but closer this time. Fargo cursed softly.

"You thinking what I am?" Robertson said.

"Yes, dammit to hell," Fargo snapped. He listened, no longer needing to strain to hear. The rifle fire was close and he picked up the other sound; hoofbeats racing up the path that passed the hollow. The captain came into sight first, his face gray with fear and strain, a small trickle of blood from a scrape along his temple. The senator and Olive were next, and then the column. But only half of it, Fargo saw. The captain came abreast of the hollow, stared at the three figures and reined to a halt.

"My God," Ellwood said as the senator halted. "We'll have to cut them loose."

"No," the senator said. "Leave them for the Mescalero. That might satisfy them, along with the troopers they've already killed. They'll stop to kill them, at least. It'll give us more time."

Fargo saw Capt. Ellwood waver, his eyes going to the senator and back to the three figures on the ground.

"Let's go, dammit, Ellwood. This is no time to get soft," the senator shouted. "We're better off with them dead anyway." He slapped his horse and raced on, and Fargo saw the captain pull the reins of his mount and follow. Olive raced by, her eyes focused straight ahead. The remains of the column followed, men too shaken and full of fear to think of anything more than escaping with their lives.

"Shit," Downs said.

"My sentiments exactly," Fargo agreed. A scraping sound caught his ears and he glanced up to see blond hair appear from the top of the nearby rocks, send the big gray down a perilously steep crevice to emerge at the hollow. She leapt from the horse, started to tear at knots.

"There's no time for that. My right calf, get the knife there," Fargo said. Blossom pushed his trouser leg up and pulled the double-edged knife from the sheath. She slashed at the ropes, used both edges of the blade in upward and downward motions. "Your conscience bother you?" Fargo asked.

"I heard the attack below," she said as she severed the last rope. "I went to look and saw the Mescalero chasing the captain and his troopers, cutting them to pieces. When I saw him head up for the foothills, I started back for you."

Fargo shook away the rope and dived for his Colt just as the Mescalero appeared. He swung one arm out, knocking Blossom on her side as an arrow pierced the air just over her head. Downs and Robertson had seized their guns and were rolling for cover, he saw.

Fargo half-dived, half-scooted behind a rock,

dragging Blossom along with him as two arrows splintered on the stone inches from his face. She got to her feet with him as he raced up a little path, pausing to peer down through a crevice to see the Mescalero halt and drop from their ponies, bows and lances in hand. He counted ten and surmised they had lost a few attacking the column. One—a thin, wiry figure, barechested and wearing a leather wrist band—directed the others with hand motions, and Fargo watched the Apache fan out and begin climbing the rocks.

Downs and Robertson had taken cover and were lying low, he noted, someplace a little below the hollow. But the Mescalero were coming up the rocks after him, and he yanked at Blossom again, climbed up higher, and found another crevice that gave him a wide view of the area. He dropped low, Blossom beside him, and raised the Colt as he saw two of the Apache come into sight, moving cautiously. They'd pinpoint his position if he fired, but he had no choice. They'd close in on him anyway, he knew. He pressed the trigger, and the two Apache fell from the rocks as if they were one. The Colt was still aimed at the spot as another Apache raced out, bow drawn. Fargo fired as the Indian let the arrow fly. The heavy .45 slug hit the bow, snapped it in two, and drove the top half of it into the man's chest as it sped on. The arrow flew harmlessly skyward and Fargo saw the Indian sink to the ground, half the bow embedded in his chest as though it were some strange tombstone.

Fargo dropped as three arrows smashed into the stone beside him, and he felt the trickle of blood from his forehead as a splinter slashed into him. He glimpsed the three Apache above him on the rocks, drawing their bows again to fire another volley into the crevice. The flurry of shots exploded from the rocks just below the hollow and Fargo saw one of the

Apache topple as the other two flung themselves low and disappeared from sight.

"Downs and Robertson," he said to Blossom. "Probably the first clear shot they had. They couldn't have picked a better time." He lifted himself up and peered down, glimpsed the two Pinkerton men scrambling for better cover below. He also saw four Apache darting down the rock-strewn slope after them. He grimaced as he counted aloud. "We got four," he muttered. "There are four more chasing down after Downs and Robertson. That leaves two." He peered out of the crevice cautiously, scanned the terrain just below, and saw nothing. "Let's go, we can't stay here," he said, rose to a crouch with Blossom at his heels as he climbed up the crevice. He reached the end, halted, felt the uneasiness pull at him. Three shots erupted from the rocks below. Downs and Robertson were having their own problems.

A ledge of rock protruded above the end of the crevice at the right. A flat-sided rock rose some eight feet high at the left. It was a devil's choice, but he decided on the ledge. "You stay here," he said to Blossom. His finger on the trigger of the Colt, he moved out of the crevice, his gaze fastened on the ledge above. Nothing showed, nothing moved. He spun, peered up at the top of the other rock. Nothing appeared there either, and he cursed silently. They were waiting somewhere else. They knew he'd come out expecting they'd be there, and so they waited. He'd seen them use the technique before; let their quarry keep expecting until he was wound up so tight he fired at shadows. Then they struck, when nerves and frustration had done half the work for them.

Fargo turned, beckoned to Blossom, and she came out. He ran across the hillside, Blossom at his heels. He wouldn't let them play their game on him. He kept running, dodged down one narrow stone fracture, then another, worked his way upward again. Suddenly he halted, yanked Blossom down beside him.

He heard the scrape along the line of rocks just above and to his left, and he turned, lifted himself up in time to see the Apache. He fired and the Indian flung himself sideways, and Fargo saw the shot chip pieces of stone away and he cursed.

"Fargo!" Blossom's scream pierced the air, and he didn't try to spin around. He threw himself forward and felt the arrow graze the side of his thigh. He rolled headlong, heard two more arrows hiss over his head, and came up against a tall rock with a crash that seemed to shake his bones loose. He felt his head swimming, pulled himself to one knee, and shook the fog from his eyes. Blossom's scream stabbed into him and he looked up to see the Mescalero holding the knife at her breast as he held her from behind. Fargo's eyes found the second Apache, only a few feet from him, bow drawn, arrow aimed at his heart. Fargo rose to his feet slowly and tossed the Colt on the ground. The Apache with Blossom marched her down the hillside. Fargo could see he was the thin, wiry one with the leather wrist band. The Indian kept his hold on Blossom as he stopped alongside Fargo and he saw the other Apache swing in on the other side of him. He had lowered his bow and he pointed downward.

Fargo started to walk between the two Apaches, the thin, wiry one holding Blossom with the knife point resting at the very tip of her breast. Neither needed words, the message all too clear. Fargo heard two more shots from below the hollow. Downs and Robertson were still holding on, he noted with grim satisfaction. The hill grew steeper, a cover of loose pebbles over it.

Fargo felt his muscles tense, thoughts transmitting messages directly to the body. There'd be no chance once they reached the hollow. It was now or never. His eyes flicked to the knife point against Blossom's breast, glanced to the Apache on his other side. The Indian wore a hunting knife tucked in the waistband of his trousers. But if he made a move at either Apache, the knife would go into Blossom. His eyes flicked to the blade again. If Blossom dropped, the blade would miss her breasts, even if the Indian's reacted instantly. It would take split-second timing, and it still might not work. But the hollow was quickly nearing.

He tensed his muscles, watching Blossom's steps as she moved down the steep hill. He snapped into action with the twisting speed of a cougar's spring. His leg snapped out first, and he kicked Blossom's feet out from under her. She went down with a yelp, and before she hit the ground, he had spun, brought a short, looping right up into the jaw of the Indian on the other side. The man went down and Fargo dived onto him, yanked the hunting knife from his waistband, and plunged it through the Apache's abdomen to the hilt. He rolled, flung himself sideways as he heard the other Indian spring at him. The Apache, knife in hand, landed a half-inch from his head, slashed out with the blade, and Fargo had to roll away. He sprang to his feet but the thin, wiry form was already charging at him. The Apache slashed with the knife again, and Fargo felt the blade graze his abdomen as he sucked himself in. He barely managed to duck the slashing blow that instantly followed.

The thin, wiry Mescalero was as quick as a sidewinder, and Fargo saw the hate glistening in the Indian's little black eyes. He backed away, but the Mescalero came after him, the hunting knife ready to lash out in any direction. Fargo tried a feint, but the Indian almost cut his wrist off with a downward stroke of the blade. He backed off again, glimpsed Blossom on her hands and knees, the very blue eyes round with fright.

The Indian began a back-and-forth sideways dance—first left, then right—and each time he thrust forward with the knife. Fargo found himself trying to match the dance to avoid the thrusting blows. But he saw that each thrust was coming closer. He couldn't match the light deftness of the wiry figure. The Apache continued the deadly little dance and Fargo cursed silently. Suddenly, the Indian leapt forward, gave a vicious thrust, and Fargo felt the knife tear through his shirt. He twisted away, aware he had neither the room nor the speed to strike a counterblow. He saw the Indian leap after him, bring the knife down in a slashing arc, and he felt the hiss of air as the knife passed harmlessly by the back of his neck.

Fargo whirled, tried to regain his footing, and felt the little pebbles roll out from beneath his feet. His legs went out from under him and he fell on his back. Out of the corner of his eye he saw the Apache leaping at him, the knife raised, and then Fargo glimpsed the blond-haired form as it hurtled through the air to slam into the Indian's legs in a flying tackle. The Apache went down and Fargo heard his oath of surprise. Blossom still clung to the Indian's legs as the Apache twisted, started to bring the knifeblade up. Fargo dived, caught the man's wrist, bent it backward, and heard the Apache grunt in pain as the knife fell from his grip. Fargo's looping right caught him flush on the jaw and the Indian flew back out of Blossom's grip. He saw her glance up from under the thick blond hair as he stepped in front of her, bringing a left up into the Indian's face as the man started to get up.

The Apache fell back against one of the rocks, dropped his head down, and dived at the big man's legs. Fargo brought one knee up and felt the Indian's jaw smash into it. The wiry figure dropped and managed to twist away, but Fargo's arms shot out and he caught the Apache by the back of the neck. Putting the full power and weight of his hard-muscled body behind it, he slammed the Mescalero's face into the rock, once, twice, a third time, until the Apache slid to the ground, a barely alive object with what had once been a face but was now only a smashed mass of oozing red, bone and flesh.

Fargo stepped back, drew a deep breath, and his eyes found Blossom. "Thanks," he said. "He would have had me."

"A down payment. I still owe you a few," she said. He straightened, and she came to him, leaned against him, not trembling but her hands tight on his arm. Two more shots echoed from the rocks below. "My God, don't they ever quit?" Blossom said.

"We outfoxed them and outfought them on their own grounds. They want their revenge," he said. "Wait here," he told her as he climbed back up the hillside and retrieved the Colt. His eyes swept the hillside below the hollow as he started down. He moved carefully, his eyes searching for brow-banded forms. There were no more shots and he saw Downs first, pulling himself out from behind a pile of small rocks. Robertson appeared, a dozen yards to the left. Both waved at him and reached the hollow just as he did.

"I'm glad I practiced my marksmanship before I left Washington," Robertson said wearily.

"The senator was right about one thing. The Apache stopped for us, and it gave them a chance to get away," Blossom said. "They escaped by trying to sacrifice us, the bastards," she added bitterly.

The flurry of distant rifle fire exploded, echoed up into the hills, and Fargo saw Blossom frown at him.

"They didn't get away," he said. "That's why the Mescalero stopped to go after us. They were chasing the troops back to where others waited." The rifle fire sputtered suddenly, ended as abruptly as it had begun. "It's over now," Fargo said quietly. "The Mescalero have had their revenge." He walked to the Ovaro and untethered the horse. "We'll hole up down a ways till it gets dark," he said, and the others followed in silence.

He found a glen of black oak and hackberry, and they waited for the day to turn to night, each with their own thoughts, Blossom sitting close to him. He rose when the night came, and glanced at Downs and Robertson. "It's not far. Want to do some burying?" he asked.

"We should. It'd be the right thing. But I'm not of a mind to," Downs said. "They deserve what they got."

"The troopers just followed orders," Fargo reminded them gently.

Robertson got to his feet. "Let's go back. I'll sleep better for it."

Fargo led the way, the others riding close behind him. The moonlight didn't make the scene look much better, only less brutal. Olive had taken a half-dozen arrows. Capt. Ellwood and Sen. Talbot resembled pincushions. Blossom helped gather small stones, and when they were finished, they rode across the flatland under the silent moon.

"What now?" she asked.

"Joe Tortillos'," Fargo said. "We've come this far. Let's see it through."

She gave a deep sigh as she nodded, and they rode for a few hours more, camped, and were in the saddle when morning came.

They reached White Sands by the end of the day. Joe Tortillos' Trading Post had a ramshackle lodge attached for passing stage drivers, and Fargo led the way into the post. "Friend of Yuma Kelly's. We met a few years back," he said to the square-shaped man with the black hair and black handlebar mustache.

"Yes, I think I remember," Joe Tortillos said.

"The Mescalero trade anything in the last month or so?" Fargo asked. "Especially a briefcase, valise, small bag."

The man shook his head. "Mescalero haven't been in here in months. Sorry," he said.

"That makes four of us," Robertson said, and followed Fargo out. "I'm disappointed but not surprised."

"I'm mad as hell," Blossom said.

"Case closed," Downs remarked as they started to ride back across the flatland of the New Mexico Territory.

"I'm beginning to agree with Blossom, but for different reasons," Robertson said. "The captain will wind up a hero and the senator a tragic victim. That oughtn't to be."

"It won't be the first time getting killed has turned a stupid bastard into a hero," Fargo said.

"That goes for the captain, but the senator's sleazy friends will still be operating, and we go back empty-handed," Robertson said.

"But alive," Downs remarked.

"Maybe not empty-handed," Blossom said. Both Pinkerton men looked at her. "I know a lot about what Dale was doing. I even know some names. I could make a statement, testify to what I know."

"Damn, that'd be enough to get at least some of the others involved and send the rest scurrying for their holes," Downs said.

"Not for nothing," Blossom said sweetly.

"Enough to cover the mortgage money?" Downs asked.

"It's a deal," Blossom said.

"We'll be heading right back. You can come with us," Downs said.

"No. I'll be along later, in a few weeks," Blossom said, and her eyes went to Fargo. "I've a bonus to pay," she said.

"I'll see she gets back safe," Fargo said to the two Pinkerton men.

They shrugged. "We could use a few weeks to prepare affidavits and papers. We'll be looking for you, Blossom," Downs said.

She waved at them as they rode off, and Fargo swung the Ovaro in beside her.

"That bonus for me?" he asked.

"Who else?" she said, frowning.

"Thought you might've meant for yourself." He grinned.

"Bastard," she said. "But then again, maybe you're right."

LOOKING FORWARD!
The following is the opening section
from the next novel in the exciting
Trailsman series from Signet:

**The Trailsman #44:
SCORPION TRAIL**

1862—Deep in the Superstition Mountains,
where the Apache's lance and the scorpion's
sting are no match for greed-crazed white men.

It was late in the afternoon of a miserably hot day
when Fargo rode into the sun-bleached town of
Tularo, Arizona. The broiling sun was like a heavy
hand pushing him down onto his sweaty saddle. The
Ovaro he rode had held up well so far, but the pinto's
head was beginning to droop noticeably.

As Fargo clopped down Tularo's hard-baked main
street, he passed an express office and jailhouse, a
general store, a saloon, a small restaurant, and a one-
story frame structure that for two bits a night offered a
wooden bunk, a pillow filled with hay, and maybe a
sheet. He had no trouble imagining the cubicles' filthy
blankets, broken mirrors, brown soap in sardine cans,
and water jugs crawling with roaches.

He kept going until he came to the town's livery, a
crooked, unpainted barn with a huge pile of manure in
the alley beside it. Dismounting, he led his pinto into
the barn, found an empty stall, and unsaddled him.
Instructing the stable boy to rub the Ovaro down thoroughly after watering and graining him, Fargo tossed

him a coin and left the livery. Lugging his bedroll and rifle, he crossed the street and entered the Arizona House, a three-story, wooden-frame hotel that was easily the most impressive building in Tularo.

Slapping the dust off his buckskins, Fargo held up for a minute in the small lobby. Potted palms had been placed hopefully about it, a few of them visibly wilting in the stifling heat. The cuspidors were caked brown with dried tobacco juice, and the bare floor around them was stained a rich mahogany.

The desk clerk was a surprise, he noted with pleasure.

She was a pretty, brown-eyed, deeply tanned young girl dressed with amazing decorum, considering the heat. Her opulent auburn curls were tied up into prim buns at the back of her head, and her long-sleeved dress was starched, her collar buttoned at the neck; and so high were her breasts, Fargo was certain she was wearing a corset. Though slightly dazed by the heat, she greeted him with a smile as he approached.

"A room for the night, sir?"

"Yes."

Fargo signed the register. As the girl handed him his key, he returned her smile and said, "I sure would like to scrub some of this dust off, ma'am, but I didn't see a barbershop when I rode in. You got any idea where the closest tubs are?"

"In the back room," she said. "On each floor. I'll heat the water and bring it up." A mischievous look flickered for a moment on her pretty face. "You'd be surprised how seldom we get calls for bathwater in this godforsaken place."

"I guess I would be, at that."

"Give me a few minutes, please."

"Of course. And thank you." Starting for the stairs, he paused and looked back at the girl. "I don't have a robe."

"I'll bring one."

Fargo thanked her and headed for the stairs.

The girl was waiting for him in the back room, the place dim with steam. She was still dressed in her high-necked dress, and Fargo glimpsed the tips of her patent-leather, high-button shoes peeking out from under her long woolen skirt. A large, high-backed iron tub was sitting in the center of the room, already half-filled with hot water—and on the floor beside the waiting girl were four steaming buckets. The robe she had promised him was hanging on a hook beside the door.

He closed the door behind him.

"Undress," she said, "and give me your clothes. I'll wash them and have them back dry by morning. The sun will see to that."

She made no effort to look away as Fargo pulled off his boots and socks and shrugged out of his sweat-heavy buckskins and underdrawers, nor did she comment or change her expression as she watched him stride, stark-naked, over to the tub and step gingerly into the steaming water.

Fargo almost yanked his foot back out and nearly let out a howl. Instead, he kept it in, sweat streaming down his forehead, then eased in all the way, his lean, powerfully muscled body adjusting gradually as he lowered himself silently into the near-scalding water. He felt as if he were plunging into the first ring of the Inferno, but made no comment as the girl, her sleeves rolled up and her dress now unbuttoned at the neck, lathered his face swiftly and proceeded to shave him.

171

She worked swiftly and deftly, and when she had finished, she emptied one of the buckets of steaming water over his head and shoulders.

This time, he was certain she had scalded him to death. He grabbed the sides of the tub to avoid leaping out of it. But his body adjusted to the water's temperature, and when he opened his eyes, he found the girl's face leaning close to his, the faintest suggestion of a smile on her puckish mouth as she worked with a bar of yellow soap and sponge, scrubbing at the dirt on his shoulders, arms, and chest. He began to relax, relishing each stroke of her sponge. His pores streamed perspiration and the suds filled the tub as he leaned back and closed his eyes, almost falling asleep as she continued to lave his body.

Abruptly, she began soaping his thick jet-black hair. Stinging suds flowed down his forehead into the corners of his eyes. He grimaced as the girl's strong fingers began massaging his scalp. Without warning, she shoved his head forward into the steaming, foamy water. He tried to straighten up, but she pushed his head down farther, kept him under for a moment longer, then allowed him to straighten up. As he did so, blowing like a seal, another bucket of scalding water cascaded down over him.

He gasped and fought for breath as the steam enveloped him, but she paid no heed to his discomfort, and producing a hard-bristle brush, she began scrubbing down his back. Once he had gained his breath, he relaxed as he felt the miles of sand and dirt peeling off his back and shoulders. For her part, the girl made no effort to hide her grin of pleasure while she contemplated Fargo's heavily muscled torso and massive shoulders, scrubbing over them and then down the front of him, moving for the first time well past the thick mat of short, curly hair on his chest.

As the girl scrubbed away, her fresh, round face came close to Fargo's. She smiled openly at him then, her teeth flashing brilliantly in her tanned face as her hand no longer shied away from what it found between his legs. As her swift fingers worked down into Fargo's crotch, they destroyed what little composure he had left.

She pulled away then and stood up. With the back of her hand she brushed a stray lock of hair off her damp forehead.

"Stand up," she told him, her dark eyes flashing.

Reluctantly, Fargo pushed himself to his full height. The girl did not embarrass him by commenting with word or glance on his involuntary erection. Ignoring it altogether, she busied herself in scrubbing down the small of his back, his buttocks, and the back of his legs. She was very thorough and Fargo could feel still more miles of dust peeling off, and maybe this time a good pound of skin with it.

Two more steaming buckets of hot water rinsed him, and then the girl folded a huge towel about his torso and helped him to step out of the tub. She patted him dry then, her hands playing a maddening tune over his suddenly alive body. She draped another towel over his dripping head and he rubbed his hair dry with it. He heard the door close.

She was gone.

Dressed in fresh buckskins and feeling at least five pounds lighter, Fargo left the hotel and walked down the street to the sheriff's office. The deputy, a lanky, reptilian creature, was sitting on the jailhouse porch, his chair tipped back, his long legs braced against the railing. Thumbing his hat brim off his face, he told Fargo that Sheriff Hammond was at the restaurant, eating his supper.

Fargo thanked the deputy and kept going until he came to Stella's Eats and entered. Stella was a large blonde piloting her course through the crush of tables as lightly as a gas-filled balloon. Despite the heat and the dark patches of sweat running down from under her enormous arms, she remained determinedly cheerful as she pointed out to Fargo the sheriff's table.

Hammond was eating alone, with a single-minded intensity that explained fully the flab larding his shoulders and the pasty, hanging jowls that gave his face a downcast look. His mouth full, he gestured with his fork toward a chair and continued to assault the mashed potatoes and gravy on his plate. A well-gnawed T-bone sat in a congealed red puddle alongside the potatoes. Thick slabs of buttered, homemade white bread sat on a saucer beside his coffee. Hammond finished chewing the load of potatoes he had just delivered to his mouth, and glared at Fargo.

"What's so important, mister?" he demanded. "Can't your business wait till I finish my supper?"

Fargo smiled easily, determined not to take offense. He was still feeling the effects of his soothing bath. "Sorry to bother you, Hammond, but this won't take long."

The sheriff put down his fork. Grabbing a slice of bread, he began mopping up the remains of his mashed potatoes. "Well, see that it don't."

"I understand a shipment of silver was sent through the Superstition Mountains a couple months ago and got held up, or lost, or whatever. That right?"

Hammond nodded, his piggish eyes narrowing. "If you know so much, why you got to bother me?"

Fargo leaned back and smiled. The smile was not easy. "I'm looking for a man said to be involved. He went with the mule team, but his body was not found with the others."

"Federico Silva."

"Was that his name?"

"Your hearin' all right, is it?"

"Did you know Silva?"

The sheriff shrugged. "Saw him a coupla times, I guess. Never noticed nothin' about him."

Fargo then described the man he was looking for, and asked the sheriff if he recognized him as Silva. The sheriff downed the bread and potatoes and gravy in one huge gulp, then reached for another slice of bread. "I told you. I never noticed nothin' special about Silva. Silva could be your man, I suppose, but I wouldn't want to swear on it." The sheriff mopped up the remains of the potatoes and gravy and shoved them into his mouth as dark fingers of gravy dribbled down over the rough stubble on his chin.

"You got any idea who attacked the train?" Fargo asked.

"Sure. Apache or Papagos. Take your pick."

"Did you go after the Apache to see if they got the silver?"

"You out of your head? That's Apache country, and them devils ain't half so bad as the scorpions. I'd sooner march into the bowels of hell as go after them Apache. We found what was left of the wagons, buried the bodies we found, and pulled our asses back out of there. Them damn fools should never've tried to take that shortcut through the Superstitions." He reached for a thick wedge of apple pie. "Now let me eat."

"Thank you, Sheriff," Fargo said, pushing his chair back and standing up.

Hammond's hand was reaching for his fork. For a second or two Fargo debated whether or not to shove the lawman's face down into the pie; then, with a weary shrug, he skirted the table and left the restaurant. Though he had been hungry enough when he entered the place, his interview with the sheriff had ruined his appetite.

Crossing the street to the saloon, he purchased a bottle of bourbon and proceeded to wash the dust off his tonsils. A plate of cheese and hardtack had been set out on the bar. He dined on this, then retired to a table along one wall, waiting for his irritation with the sheriff and his frustration at finding out so little about Federico Silva to burn itself out. . . .

It was dark and Fargo was close to calling it a day when a sharp cry caused him to glance over at a corner of the saloon where a poker game was in progress.

"Grab his arm," someone cried.

One of the poker players—a tin-faced bald fellow— leapt up from the table as two other players, one on each side of him, grabbed his arms. His chair striking the floor behind him sounded like a gunshot in the small saloon.

Fargo stood up and peered over the heads of the men closing about the poker players and saw the bald player attempting to claw his way free of the two men restraining him. But they held him fast, and as Fargo watched, he saw a playing card protruding from the struggling poker player's extra-wide cuff—an ace of spades.

It stood out like a wart on a whore's cheek.

The bald fellow snatched his arm back and watched in a kind of dazed horror as the ace of spades fluttered to the floor. The two men holding him let go, and as the unlucky gambler slammed back against the wall, one of the two men—a tall, cadaverous blade of a man with a drooping, tobacco-stained mustache—reached back for his six-gun.

"Stand back, Jed," the lanky man told his companion. "This cheatin' son of a bitch might have a belly gun on him."

Jed took a hasty step backward and drew his own weapon.

In desperation, the gambler flung a chair at the tall one, drew a mean little derringer from his belt, and aimed it at Jed. The two men fired simultaneously. The twin detonations thundered deafeningly as thick clouds of gunsmoke obscured the men.

Through the smoke, Fargo saw Jed drop his gun and pitch forward onto the floor. The bald gambler, his face ashen, dropped his derringer and grabbed at his right shoulder. Blood streamed through his fingers.

"Jed's gut-shot," someone cried.

The onlookers crowded closer and stared down at Jed. The doomed man was writhing in agony as blood pulsed in a black, steaming flow through his fingers. An old man knelt beside Jed, then called for a doctor. Someone near the door turned and rushed from the saloon as others, drawn by the sound of gunfire, crowded in through the batwings.

The tall fellow turned then and glared at the wounded gambler, covering him with his Colt. The bald man, still clutching at his bleeding shoulder, took a frightened step back.

"This son of a bitch swings," the tall man told those crowding around, his voice cutting like a knife through the saloon. "Someone get a rope."

There was a quick roar of agreement as two men dashed from the place.

"No," the bald gambler cried. "You've got to give me a trial. I'm a wounded man. I shot Jed in self-defense."

Harsh, contemptuous laughter greeted his assertion as quick hands reached for the hapless fellow and dragged him, still protesting, from the saloon.

Fargo followed them and saw the group heading down the street toward the livery barn.

As the tall fellow, who was now in charge, paused momentarily under a streetlamp, Fargo got a better look at him. There was not an ounce of extra tallow on the man, his rake-handle slimness making him appear even taller than his six feet. His wrists, long and slender, hung far out of his coat sleeves, and his dark eyes sat in deep hollows. It was clear he would brook no interference—and there appeared to be no one in town prepared to go against him.

Sheriff Hammond and his deputy hurried past Fargo and overtook the tall man. Pulling him around, the sheriff demanded, "what happened, John? I heard shots."

"We finally caught Percy cheatin'," John replied. "And this time, dead to rights. The son of a bitch went for his belly gun and blasted poor Jed in the gut. Jed's back there on the floor now, bleeding to death."

Hammond swallowed. "Did Jed draw on him?"

"Damn right. And so did I."

"But don't you see, John? That means Percy shot Jed in self-defense. We got to give Percy a fair trial."

"Don't give me none of that shit," John told the sheriff. "We got a job to do and you two ain't goin' to stop us."

When Hammond appeared ready to protest again, the tall fellow placed his hand on the sheriff's shoulder, spun him out of his way, and continued on after the others.

Hammond and the deputy watched him go. After a minute, both men shrugged, apparently washing their hands of the affair, and started toward Fargo on their way back to the saloon.

Fargo blocked their progress. "Sheriff, you and this here deputy goin' to let them string that feller up?"

"What's it to you, stranger?"

"I just wanted to hear you two lawmen admit it, that's all."

"Hell," Hammond blustered. "This here lynching's only savin' the taxpayers of this town an expensive trial."

Fargo looked at both men for a long moment, then brushed contemptuously past them after the mob. It had reached the stable by now, and Fargo saw a rope flung up over a beam and snaked back down to the crowd. By the time he reached the crowd milling in front of the stable, a small fellow standing under the beam had almost finished fashioning a hangman's noose from one end of the rope.

The gambler Percy—his face a pale, quivering mask of terror—was being held upright by three men, two at his side and one just behind him. Blood was still seeping from his shoulder wound, but no one paid any attention to it. Fargo wondered how in hell they intended to get the poor son of a bitch up onto the horse.

"Hey, Carswell," someone called to the tall man. "You goin' to do the honors?"

John Carswell nodded emphatically and spat a gob of tobacco juice onto the ground beside him. "Since it was Jed this bastard killed," he barked, "I'd consider it a pleasure."

Everyone stepped back to let Carswell move closer. Percy, close to sobbing out his terror by this time, shrank back in horror as Carswell strode toward him.

"Mount up, you son of a bitch," Carswell told him.

"I can't," Percy quavered. "I'm hurt bad."

"That so?" inquired Carswell comically, cocking an eyebrow as he glanced around at his audience. "Well, now, you can relax, Percy. This rope's just the medicine for you. In a few minutes, I guarantee you won't feel a thing."

There was a howl of laughter from the crowd as Carswell clapped a bony claw of a hand on Percy's good shoulder and hauled him over toward the horse.

"Hold it right there," Fargo told him, stepping between Carswell and the horse. "Maybe you better think this over, Carswell."

Carswell peered in startled surprise at Fargo. "Get the hell out of my way, stranger!"

Fargo smiled coldly, but did not move. "This is murder. I saw the whole thing. This man has a trial due him."

"Who the hell dealt you into this?" Carswell demanded furiously.

"I did," Fargo told him quietly.

With a sudden sweep of his arm, Carswell shoved Fargo violently to one side, then told the fellow who had fashioned the hangman's noose to throw it over to him. As soon as Carswell caught it, he dropped it over the gambler's head and was about to boost the terrified gambler up onto the horse when Fargo rested the muzzle of his Colt against Carswell's temple.

Carswell froze.

"Now," Fargo told him quietly, "you just tell these assholes to go on home to their beds or back to the saloon."

Astounded at Fargo's action, the crowd shrank back. Carswell took a deep breath and turned his head cautiously to face Fargo, who poked the barrel up under Carswell's chin and smiled.

"You'll regret this," Carswell said, his narrow face dark with fury.

"I'd regret it a whole lot more if I stood by and let you bravos hang this here gambler. You know damn well it was self-defense. Both you men drew on him."

"All I know for sure, you big son of a bitch, is you better not let this four-flusher escape this rope."

"Tell the crowd to back off."

Carswell held up a moment, his malevolent dark eyes measuring Fargo's determination. What he saw in Fargo's cold lake-blue eyes convinced him.

"All right, boys," he cried, "back off."

"And give me that rope."

Carswell handed it to Fargo, who lifted it off the trembling gambler's neck and flung it away. The fellow still holding Percy released him and stepped hastily back.

Percy should have collapsed to the ground from loss of blood. Instead, the moment he felt himself no longer under constraint, he summoned his remaining strength and bolted through the thinning crowd, knocking over a youngster in his haste to get away. Once in the clear, he started racing down the street with an amazing burst of speed.

"He's escapin'," Carswell thundered.

At once, six-guns thundered as a rapid volley of fire erupted from the crowd, shattering windows, springing leaks in barrels, and causing horses to shy and break away in terror from the hitching racks. Not twenty yards from the stable, the fleeing gambler staggered, then crumpled to the ground, his bleeding carcass jolting with each round's impact.

Slowly, wearily, Fargo holstered his weapon.

Carswell did the same, then turned to face Fargo. "You better not be thinkin' of stayin' in this town, mister."

"I'll be stayin' as long as I please."

"Yeah? Well, the next time you draw on me, you better be prepared to pull the trigger."

Fargo tipped his head and smiled. "Hell, Carswell, what makes you think I wasn't prepared to do it this time?" Turning, Fargo pushed his way through the crowd. He could feel Carswell's cold eyes boring into his back, but he did not pause or look around once as he mounted the hotel's porch and went inside.

An aged cowpoke with sad eyes and gaunt features was hurrying around behind the front desk. It was clear the fellow had abandoned his post to watch the excitement outside. He stared at Fargo cautiously as Fargo asked him where the other desk clerk, the girl, had gone.

"You mean Mrs. Poole?"

"If that's her name."

"She ain't no desk clerk." He sniffed and sent a dark stream of chewing tobacco into a cuspidor at his right. "That's Emma Poole. She's the owner."

Fargo frowned. "A young girl—all done up in starched woolen dress and patent-leather shoes?"

"You want Mrs. Poole should go around in pants?"

Fargo shrugged. "Sorry," he said, then asked for the key to his room.

He was suddenly very tired.

Not long after, a somewhat depleted bottle of bourbon on the floor beside him, Fargo lay on his bed staring up at a crack in the ceiling as he gloomily pondered the day's adventures.

He had not exactly covered himself with glory. His foolhardy attempt to stop the lynching had only made the sheriff and his deputy look bad and turned a stranger into an implacable foe. The moment that damn fool of a gambler got his ass blown off, the joke was on Fargo.

Fargo shook his head. Served him right for meddling. It was always a bad idea. Maybe someday he would learn. If he lived that long.

He was reaching for the bourbon when someone knocked lightly on his door. Since he did not know anyone in town—not any that were friendly, that is—he reached swiftly under the pillow for his Colt and swung off the bed.

The light rap came again.

On bare feet he padded across the room and flattened himself against the wall beside the door. "Who is it?"

"Me."

Fargo recognized the voice at once. Mrs. Poole. He turned the key in the lock and opened the door. She stepped quickly inside. Her thick, auburn hair was combed out now and she looked about five pounds lighter, even though she was still wearing the high-necked, long-sleeved dress.

Fargo closed the door behind her. "What can I do for you, ma'am?"

She looked at the gun in his hand. "First, you can put away that cannon." She smiled. "I assure you, I come in peace."

"That's good to know," Fargo replied. He walked over to the bed and placed the Colt under the pillow. When he turned to look back at her, she was reaching behind her, unbuttoning the back of her dress and watching him, her lower lip full and moist, her eyes dusky with desire.

"I just thought I'd finish what I started," she said.

As her dress dropped to the floor, Fargo saw that she had made things easy for them both. She wore no corset or underclothes, not even a chemise. She stepped out of her slippers and strode boldly toward him. The dress had hid a lot—two saucy, upthrusting breasts with dark-pink nipples erect and ready, a waist so narrow he could span it with his hands, and her dark, gleaming pubic patch between smooth white thighs.

In his haste to strip off his long johns, he almost knocked over the bourbon, and he was naked by the time she reached him. He opened his arms to her. She moved closer to him, pressing herself against his stiffness. He grabbed her buttocks and pulled her hard against him. Like a key going into a lock, he entered her. He felt as if his cock were inside a furnace as she thrust her pelvis hungrily forward and flung her head back.

"Ever since this afternoon," she breathed, "I've been thinking of you. And all that . . . equipment."

"Is that why you left so quick?"

"What do you think?"

She ground her pubis into him, then leaned forward to press her breasts against his chest, letting her hair cascade down his back as she wrapped her arms about him.

"This is what I think," he said, swinging her gently onto the bed. Rolling on top of her, he kept himself inside her, but held back from thrusting, savoring the feel of her hot muff tight around his erection and contenting himself for the moment by worrying her nipples with his tongue and teeth until they had grown so hard they were like hot nails.

Then he let his lips travel up to her neck and move behind her ears, nibbling for a while on each lobe. She was breathing heavily, frantically, as he closed his lips over hers and thrust his tongue deep into her mouth. Their tongues, hot and wanton, clashed wildly, feverishly.

She began to thrash and undulate under him.

But still he did not thrust as he kept her impaled beneath him, pinned to the bed, fighting her desperate desire to begin the thrusting. At last, she pulled her lips away from his.

"You bastard," she cried fiercely.

Laughing, he pulled back. "What's the matter?"

"You know damn well." She blew a wet lock of hair out of her eyes. "Get on with it. I can hardly move."

He reached under her buttocks and lifted her off the bed, ramming her up at him. Then he dropped her, allowing himself to slip out completely.

"No," she groaned, gasping. "Stay in."

"Make up your mind."

"Damn you," she cried, arching up desperately to meet him.

By then he, too, was no longer interested in prolonging things. Recklessly, he plunged down into her, this time hitting bottom as she grunted and drove back up against him like a coiled spring, meeting him thrust for thrust.

"Good," she muttered. "Yes, yes."

Still thrusting, he reared upright, watching her fingers clutching at the blanket, her head turned to one side. He could see her mouth open and slack, her face pressing against the blanket with each heaving lunge, her eyes wide and staring.

He slowed then, teasing her again, moving back when she moved forward, denying her what she wanted.

"You bastard," she snarled again, looking back up at him.

Reaching up, she flung both arms around his neck, pulling him down onto her so she could claw his back raw. He loved the feeling of her fingers on his back and resumed humping her with a happy, wild abandon.

"Keep going," she whimpered. "Please. Don't stop."

This time he had no intention of stopping as he caught a glimpse of her breasts jiggling, saw her head straining back, her neck taut, her mouth open, and he felt his orgasm surging up relentlessly within him. At last he exploded inside her, pulsing wildly until, spent, he fell forward onto her breasts.

She shuddered beneath him and bucked like a bronc as she also came. When she finally went limp, he pulled her over onto her side and with his big hands on her buttocks, pressed himself into her, ramming as deep as he could go so that he would not lose his erection.

Gasping, she flung her arms about him and squeezed him tightly, and a moment later he could feel her trembling all over as she built to another climax . . . and another . . .

When finally their hard breathing subsided, they found themselves covered with a fine film of perspiration. The chill desert air was blowing in through the open window, so Fargo pulled a sheet over them both. He reached down for the bourbon.

"I could use some of that too," she said.

He pulled on the bottle a couple of times, then

handed it to her. Wiping off the bottle's mouth with her palm, she took a healthy belt and handed it back to Fargo.

As he put it back down on the floor, she propped her head up on an elbow and peered at him, a mischievous gleam in her eyes. "I saw you out there tangling with Big John."

"That what they call Carswell?"

"Yep."

"Made a fool of myself."

"You were the only one who tried to do the right thing. It took guts."

He looked at her. She dressed like a lady, fucked like a wildcat, and talked like a man. He shrugged. "That poor son of a bitch made it easy for everyone, I guess, when he broke away like that."

"You plannin' on staying in these parts, Skye?"

"Nope."

"What brought you here in the first place?"

Fargo told her he was looking for a man called Silva, who he figured might have been mixed up in the attack on the mule team a couple of months ago in the Superstition Mountains.

"I remember Silva," she said. "He stayed at the hotel, but I didn't see much of him. He left with the mule team."

"The sheriff said he wasn't found with the others. Said he disappeared."

"He could have wandered off after the attack, wounded."

"Maybe."

"If he did, he wouldn't last long in that country."

"That ain't what I was thinkin'. Silva might've been in on that raid. And that could mean he's just the one I'm looking for."

"Why are you after him, Skye? You ain't no lawman."

"Old business. There's four men I took after some time ago—for what they did to my ma and pa. Now there's just two left."

"And you're hopin' this is one of them."

Fargo nodded.

She looked at him for a long moment. "I see."

"You think I'm crazy?"

She shrugged. "You can spend your time playing pinochle with grizzly bears for all I care." She snuggled closer. "Say, where'd you get that funny half-moon scar on your arm?"

He grinned at her. "Playin' pinochle with grizzly bears."

"Be serious."

"I am. Almost. I got in a ruckus with a full-grown grizzly once. I was lucky I got away."

She shuddered and snuggled still closer. He let her snuggle and asked how she became the owner of a hotel in the middle of Apache country.

She told him. The hotel's original owner had given it to her father in payment for his silver mine. The silver petered out not more than a few weeks after they signed the papers, making it the only good bargain she remembered her father ever having made. When her father died a year later, he left the hotel in her name.

"So now you're stuck here?"

"You want to buy this place?"

"Not on your life."

"Then I guess you're right. I'm stuck here."

Fargo felt himself rising to the occasion once again. He must have been hornier than he realized. Too damn many days on the trail alone.

"Skye?"

"What is it, Emma?"

"I don't think you should've got John Carswell all riled up like you did."

"Any special reason why not?"

"He might know something about Silva—or at least what happened to him."

"How so?"

"There's talk around that he had something to do with that lost silver shipment. One of his boys got drunk a few nights back and opened his mouth. His brother shut him up fast enough, but it's got some people in town talking. If Carswell *was* mixed up with that holdup, then maybe he would know what happened to Silva."

Fargo sat up and looked down at Emma Poole. "You might have something there. Carswell live in town?"

"No. He's a rancher, way out by Clay Springs, right close to the Superstition Mountains—and the Apaches."

"Ain't that a mite dangerous?"

"For the Apaches, maybe. That Carswell clan is wild, Skye I wouldn't trust a single one of them. There's a passel of them, too—and they're as close as ticks on a hound dog."

"Where's this Clay Springs?"

"Under the Mogollon Rim next to the desert."

"How can they make a living runnin' cattle on that kind of land?"

"That's what a lot of people wonder. But they manage somehow."

"And maybe hitting a few pack trains might be one way."

"I didn't say that."

"But a lot of people are thinkin' that."

"Yes."

"I think maybe I'll take a ride out to Clay Springs, Emma."

"Not right now."

"No," he said, sinking down beside her. "Not right now."

She smiled and, reaching down to his crotch, closed her hand around his resurgent erection. Her eyes widened in pleased astonishment.

"Now it's *my* turn to devil you," she told him, swinging one long limb over his waist.

"Go ahead. You've earned the right."

"You bet I have," she said, swinging the other leg over him.

Fargo said nothing as she rammed herself down as hard as she could onto his erection. He leaned back and prepared to enjoy himself. He had a long ride ahead of him the next day, but there was no way he would be able to leave first thing in the morning—not even if he wanted to. He was going to have too busy a night.

Not that he was complaining.

Exciting Westerns by Jon Sharpe from SIGNET

(0451)

☐ THE TRAILSMAN #1: SEVEN WAGONS WEST   (127293—$2.50)
☐ THE TRAILSMAN #2: THE HANGING TRAIL   (110536—$2.25)
☐ THE TRAILSMAN #3: MOUNTAIN MAN KILL   (121007—$2.50)
☐ THE TRAILSMAN #4: THE SUNDOWN SEARCHERS   (122003—$2.50)
☐ THE TRAILSMAN #5: THE RIVER RAIDERS   (127188—$2.50)
☐ THE TRAILSMAN #6: DAKOTA WILD   (119886—$2.50)
☐ THE TRAILSMAN #7: WOLF COUNTRY   (123697—$2.50)
☐ THE TRAILSMAN #8: SIX-GUN DRIVE   (121724—$2.50)
☐ THE TRAILSMAN #9: DEAD MAN'S SADDLE   (126629—$2.50)
☐ THE TRAILSMAN #10: SLAVE HUNTER   (114655—$2.25)
☐ THE TRAILSMAN #11: MONTANA MAIDEN   (116321—$2.25)
☐ THE TRAILSMAN #12: CONDOR PASS   (118375—$2.50)
☐ THE TRAILSMAN #13: BLOOD CHASE   (119274—$2.50)
☐ THE TRAILSMAN #14: ARROWHEAD TERRITORY   (120809—$2.50)
☐ THE TRAILSMAN #15: THE STALKING HORSE   (121430—$2.50)
☐ THE TRAILSMAN #16: SAVAGE SHOWDOWN   (122496—$2.50)
☐ THE TRAILSMAN #17: RIDE THE WILD SHADOW   (122801—$2.50)
☐ THE TRAILSMAN #18: CRY THE CHEYENNE   (123433—$2.50)
☐ THE TRAILSMAN #19: SPOON RIVER STUD   (123875—$2.50)
☐ THE TRAILSMAN #20: THE JUDAS KILLER   (124545—$2.50)
☐ THE TRAILSMAN #21: THE WHISKEY GUNS   (124898—$2.50)
☐ THE TRAILSMAN #22: THE BORDER ARROWS   (125207—$2.50)
☐ THE TRAILSMAN #23: THE COMSTOCK KILLERS   (125681—$2.50)
☐ THE TRAILSMAN #24: TWISTED NOOSE   (126203—$2.50)

Prices higher in Canada

JOIN THE *TRAILSMAN* READERS' PANEL

Help us bring you more of the books you like by filling out this survey and mailing it in today.

1. Book Title: _____

   Book #: _____

2. Using the scale below, how would you rate this book on the following features? Please write in one rating from 0-10 for each feature in the spaces provided.

POOR	NOT SO GOOD		O.K.			GOOD		EXCEL-LENT	
0	1	2	3	4	5	6	7	8	9	10

                                                                RATING

Overall opinion of book .... _____

Plot/Story .... _____

Setting/Location .... _____

Writing Style .... _____

Character Development .... _____

Conclusion/Ending .... _____

Scene on Front Cover .... _____

3. About how many western books do you buy for yourself each month? _____

4. How would you classify yourself as a reader of westerns? I am a (   ) light (   ) medium (   ) heavy reader.

5. What is your education?
   (   ) High School (or less) (   ) 4 yrs. college
   (   ) 2 yrs. college   (   ) Post Graduate

6. Age _____   7. Sex: (   ) Male (   ) Female

Please Print Name_____

Address_____

City _____ State _____ Zip _____

Phone # (   )_____

Thank you. Please send to New American Library, Research Dept., 1633 Broadway, New York, NY 10019.